ONCE UPON A TIME

City girl Meredith plans to write a novel in the peace and quiet of the country, but finds her chosen retreat is overrun by a film production company. Despite her best intentions, she is soon lured from her storytelling into a make-believe world of early Australia, with handsome, bearded bushrangers on horseback, and women in long skirts, boots and gingham bonnets. But in the real world, a little girl is in danger . . .

46

ZELMA FALKINER

ONCE UPON A TIME

Complete and Unabridged

LINFORD
Leicester

First published in Great Britain in 2005

First Linford Edition
published 2009

British Library CIP Data

Falkiner, Zelma.
  Once upon a time- -
  (Linford romance library)
  1. Motion picture locations- -Fiction.
  2. Fiction- -Authorship- -Fiction.
  3. Romantic suspense novels.
  4. Large type books.
  I. Title II. Series
  823.9'2–dc22

  ISBN 978–1–84782–865–1

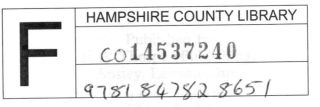

Printed and bound in Great Britain by
T. J. International Ltd., Padstow, Cornwall

This book is printed on acid-free paper

1

The road through the tunnel of tall trees ended at a gate hung with a faded sign. If one could call it a gate, marvelled Meredith, getting out from the car to examine it more closely.

Misshapen sticks and twisted wire had been randomly woven into a makeshift barrier. A heavy chain padlocked it to a thick tree-trunk.

Carefully, so as not to chip her immaculate scarlet nail polish, she inserted the key in the rusty lock and turned it. Before she could step out of the way, the chain and lock slipped from her hands, dragging everything down with it, and the gate collapsed across the latest addition to her wardrobe of imported shoes.

She didn't know whether to laugh or cry. It had become that kind of a day. The long drive from the city was trouble-free and had gone quickly enough. Until she left the highway.

From then on, travelling the meandering back roads required many stops to map-read, as well as more careful driving. Not what she was used to at all.

When at last she drove into the valley township that was her destination, Meredith was tired and ready for lunch. For half-an-hour she had been teasing her taste-buds with the possibilities of the menu.

On work days, lunch was always a pleasurable occasion. After her usual breakfast of a snatched cup of take-away coffee from the kiosk on the way through to the elevators, she looked forward to it.

Would she order a smoke salmon bagel, with cream cheese and capers today or a sandwich of rye bread generously filled with oven-roasted vegetables? What about rare roast beef and plenty of horseradish? On multi-grain bread.

Still undecided, Meredith pulled into

the gutter, parked and got out.

The short street lay somnolent in the midday sun. Nothing stirred behind the closed shop-fronts, each with trading hours clearly marked. The bakery, the cafe, even the garage, took a two-hour break. Meredith couldn't believe her eyes. Two hours? Was there no assistance to be given to the passing traveller?

Obviously there never were any passing travellers, this was the end of the line, a place where time stood still. Just what she said she wanted, but it would take a little getting used to. In all her planning she hadn't considered being without city amenities such as staggered lunch hours. Or the lack of even a previously scorned, coin-operated coffee machine serving a revolting brew.

Something moved on a bench beneath a shady tree on the median strip and attracted her attention. Pleased by this sign of life in an otherwise deserted landscape, Meredith picked her way across the road and addressed the prone figure.

'Excuse me, could you tell me where I could get coffee and something to eat?'

A muffled voice came from under a white-brimmed hat. 'The cafe, at two o'clock.'

Meredith reined in her irritation. 'That's almost an hour and a half. Isn't there somewhere I could at least get a cup of coffee before then?' she asked. 'A machine, perhaps?'

A hand went up to lazily lift the hat. She found herself being examined by two brown eyes, two youngish brown eyes, despite the bearded face, she noted. Beards tended to give maturity to a face, she always thought.

'An impatient city-slicker,' the man remarked drily, letting the hat drop back to put an end to her observations.

She was used to people taking notice when she asked a question — it was the way in business. This was obviously some yokel who hadn't heard of good manners.

Yet there was nothing about the man's appearance to suggest that.

On the contrary, the beard, though longish, was neatly trimmed, what she had seen of it, the clothes were definitely up-market country casual, the boots on the end of long legs, a recognisable well-known brand. What was he doing lying on a bench in the empty street?

'Yes, I'm from the city,' she admitted defensively, then tried to claw back the initiative. 'Does that make any difference when one needs a cup of coffee?' she asked icily.

Slowly the figure lowered his feet to the ground and twisted his body into an upright position. The likelihood of anyone mistaking him for a tramp or a layabout disappeared when he stood up.

He had the bearing of a confident man, lord of all he surveyed. Handsome though he was, Meredith took an instant dislike to him.

The midday sun highlighted the

reddish tinges to the thick head of hair as he bowed low with a flourish of his hat.

'Indeed it does, m'am,' he answered, with an exaggerated drawl. 'City folk are particularly welcome and we do our best to please.'

'Does that welcome extend to asking the cafe to open and provide refreshments?'

He sounded shocked. 'Outside prescribed business hours? And risk prosecution by the Department of Labour? No, I'm sorry, it's out of the question.'

Government inspectors? Hadn't the news reached this part of the country? Surely he was joking. Meredith couldn't tell. Now firmly on his head, its brim pulled low, the hat hid his eyes, and a luxuriant moustache covered his mouth.

But he had given her an opening to call his bluff. 'Little chance of that,' she remarked. 'The Department was abolished years ago. The Shop Trading

Reform Act I think it was called.'

Having delivered her put-down, she looked around. What an unbelievable bore. She was stuck. No coffee, no lunch, and no hope of getting the keys and directions to the cottage from the letting agent, either.

Ignoring the man, she turned back towards her car. A drink of warm bottled water would have to do, and perhaps the glove-box contained a forgotten, calorie-laden chocolate bar.

'But if you were nice to me, Miss Gale, I would be happy to make my facilities available to give you a coffee.'

The use of her name astonished Meredith. She stopped and swung around to face him.

'How do you know my name?' she asked, glancing down at her business valise. There was no identifying tag that could have given her away.

'I was waiting for you,' he replied easily.

'Waiting for me?'

She had heard some good pick-up

lines in her time, but they were usually made in a social context. This encounter in the middle of nowhere hardly qualified as a social occasion.

'Yes, waiting for you. I don't usually lie on a bench in the street.'

Meredith wanted to walk on but her curiosity got the better of her. 'I'm pleased to hear that,' she retorted. 'But you haven't explained how you know who I am.'

There was a slight twitch of the man's beard, but if it was a smile it didn't reach his eyes. That was another thing she noticed about beards — you couldn't really see much of the face underneath. It became something of a guessing game to work out what the man was thinking. Or feeling.

He stared steadily back at her. 'We don't get many . . . ' His voice trailed off as if he was carefully selecting a word. 'Visitors,' he finished. 'Now, if you'll come over to my office, I'll make you a cup of coffee.'

It still didn't answer her question, but

she decided that could wait. He had hesitated before using the word visitors. What other word had he intended to use and thought better of?

'Are you sure this won't be breaking any local laws?' she asked spikily, then bit her tongue. It wouldn't do to antagonise the man before he made good on his offer of coffee, she really was desperate for a caffeine lift.

The snide remark didn't seem to upset him. He laughed and led the way across the street.

He pushed open an unpainted door that led on to a narrow walkway between a hardware store and a hairdresser's premises. To Meredith, it seemed an uninviting entrance to an office, and in the absence of a sign, certainly not likely to catch any passing trade.

She pulled herself up. Coming from the city, it was hard to get used to the idea there would be no passing trade in this town. She wondered what kind of a business the man conducted, probably a solicitor. If one could judge from his appearance, it paid well.

Intrigued, despite herself, she followed.

The alleyway ended with another door, this time more substantial, and locked. Suddenly, they were in a yard neatly stacked with timber, plastic sacks of fertiliser and a variety of gardening implements.

The man led the way into a cluttered office at the back of the hardware store and motioned Meredith toward a spare chair. She looked about her, hurriedly revising her opinion as to his occupation.

Was she going to be offered instant coffee made with hot water from the battered electric kettle almost covered by the business papers on the desk? She tried not to shudder.

Her host moved to a cupboard and pulled back the folding doors to reveal a small Italian coffee-making machine.

Surprised and relieved, Meredith broke the silence with a question.

'Are you going to tell me how you knew my name?' she asked. Before he could answer, another question followed, as was her nature. 'And what did you mean by saying you were waiting for me? Perhaps you could begin with who you are.'

'Expresso or cappuccino?'

'Expresso, thank you.'

He made no attempt to continue with the conversation.

Soon the rich aroma of the beans tantalised her taste-buds. Only after Meredith had taken her first sip, sighed her approval and relaxed back in her chair did he show signs of having heard her questions.

Leaning forward across the desk with hand outstretched, he introduced himself.

'I'm Robert Hurst — '

'The letting agent?'

'Yes. I was expecting you.'

'But what are you doing in a hardware store?'

'I'm running it, and real estate

matters are a sideline. We have the post office agency and also carry fishing bait, both of which you'll be able to avail yourself of in time.'

The beard moved again and there was a flash of white teeth as Robert Hurst laughed at his little joke. It was unlikely she would need fishing bait and he knew it.

'Coffee to your liking?'

'Perfect,' she replied honestly.

'Good. Now, to business. You'll be anxious to get out to the farmhouse and settle in. I put together a starter kit for the kitchen in case you arrived, as you did, during the lunch break.' He waved towards a box by the door.

Meredith was beginning to regard Robert Hurst in a new light. This certainly was no country hick. He appreciated good coffee and had thought of everything. For some reason it irritated her; that was usually her role — Meredith Gale, wonderwoman.

'I'll have to wait until the cafe opens, for my lunch,' she said, thinking she'd found a chink in his armour.

He got up from his chair and lifted the box of supplies on to the desk.

'I've taken the liberty of choosing a sandwich and some pieces of fruit for you,' he said, holding up a large brown paper bag.

Meredith could feel her irritation rising again. This man was too good to be true. Was he trying to make a point? She couldn't tell what was going on behind the beard.

'Thank you. I'll be on my way then.'

He handed over a sheet of paper and bulky envelope.

'Your rental contract and the keys. There's no need to lock up around here but you, being from the city, probably won't believe that. The larger one is for the gate. This street veers to the right to become Glen Road. Just follow it until you reach the very end. As the name says, it's about a mile in the old measurements.' He picked up the box of supplies. 'I'll carry these to your car.'

It was hard to fault him. That is, until she reached the gate at Mile End . . .

He could have at least warned me, she grumbled to herself as she awkwardly dragged the tangle of wire and sticks out of the way and drove through.

★　★　★

The farmhouse was small but neat and, from the outside, quite appealing with its backdrop of gentle foothills. An outdoor lounger swung invitingly from the branch of an old jacaranda tree in the garden. It would be just the place to have her lunch, she decided.

Balancing the box of supplies on one hip, Meredith put the key in the front door lock and entered the house that was to be her home for the next three months.

The hallway, freshly-painted buttercup yellow, led into a simply furnished sitting room of the same shade. Yellow brightened the two bedrooms on the cooler side of the house, and was repeated in the bathroom.

She wasn't surprised to find the kitchen had been painted from the same can, but with cupboard doors picked out in a vivid blue. She wondered if yellow was the preferred colour in the district. Or had the hardware shop secured a job-lot at a good price from the paint manufacturers?

Whatever, she had to admit the whole effect was cheery, old-fashioned but quite livable, she supposed, trying not to think of her habourside apartment.

Picking up the brown paper bag that held her lunch, she made her way back into the garden. She brushed the last of the purple spring flowering from the seat and sat down.

Robert Hurst had surprised her again. The bag contained a half bottle of red wine, uncorked and recorked, wrapped in a linen napkin and topped by an inverted glass. Another napkin kept a sandwich separate from a bunch of plump grapes, a polished apple and a cheese plate covered by cling-film. The bread was homemade and crusty, filled with lashings of shaved ham. A perfect picnic lunch, she decided as she tasted Dijon mustard on her tongue with the first bite.

Meredith had to admit the bearded manager of the hardware store was an enigma. What was a sophisticated man like him doing in this rural backwater? If he was a local landowner, what was he doing in a store? And why was such a fashion-conscious man still wearing a hippie beard?

Meredith knew answers to her questions would not be forthcoming — they wouldn't be asked. She wasn't in the country to socialise with the locals, but to prove she could write a novel.

As personal assistant to the head of a publishing firm, she had nursed a secret desire to be a published author. She was sure time was the missing ingredient. The wish lay dormant as she organised the television appearances, book launchings and literary luncheons to promote writers and their books.

No-one knew of the dream. She kept it to herself until, after ten years in her demanding job, accrued long-service meant she could follow that dream. A lot of thought had gone into finding a suitably out-of-the-way place, the idea being to have as little distraction as possible without being completely cut off from civilisation.

Although she'd been surprised to discover just how time had passed by her chosen destination, Robert Hurst's e-mailed reply to her letter of enquiry was no surprise. Everyone had a computer nowadays.

Thinking of computers, Meredith was reminded of her own equipment carefully packed in the car. Refreshed by her lunch, she began the task of moving it into the cottage.

She decided the smaller bedroom

would easily convert into a workman-like office. Its french windows overlooked green pastures that began beyond the garden fence and met the surrounding foothills without presenting anything to divert a writer.

By the end of the day, Meredith was ready for her new life. But Robert Hurst proved right again.

As darkness enveloped the country-side, she felt the city need to lock the front and back doors before preparing a meal of bacon and eggs. This was followed by a long soak in the deep, claw-footed bath. When she emerged from the steamy room, every muscle relaxed, she expected to fall asleep as soon as she got into bed.

Hours later, she was still restlessly turning. It wasn't because the bed was uncomfortable. In fact, she found it just the opposite. There was nothing wrong with the pillows, either. She supposed her landlord was responsible. He had, with his usual flair, supplied the cottage with top-class bedding.

But without the familiar hum of city traffic as background, the silence of the country night was unnerving. Every noise that broke it was magnified and jerked her back into full wakefulness.

The timber cottage creaked as it cooled. The forgotten sounds stirred childhood memories of lying awake, night after night, listening for her father's return and the inevitable arguments that would result.

Aware there would be no sleep at all if she allowed herself to go down that path, Meredith deliberately switched her thoughts to her proposed novel, escaping into the make-believe world of fiction that she planned to write about.

But there were other noises, sometimes distant, sometimes seeming to be outside her window, that were beyond such easy identification. They swept her back into the present, setting her nerves quivering.

Once she got up and, without switching on a lamp, went to the window and stared out into the darkness. Not a light was visible, just blackness. Who could say what or who lay out there?

The possibilities threatened to over-whelm her. How could she live here? Even as she asked herself that, she knew the answer. She had to get on top of the fear before it undermined her confidence and she had to flee back to the city. Admitting defeat was not easy for her to do.

A new, more insistent noise demanded her attention. What could it be? Some-thing, someone scratching to get in? It was a stupid thought. Turning on lights as she went, Meredith forced herself to go from room to room, following the sound to its source. Soon the whole house was reassuringly ablaze.

The rectangle of light from the kitchen window reached no further than the shrubbery growing up against the house. Bushes swayed to and fro in the rising wind, their hard branches scraping against the wall.

Mocking herself for being frightened by such a simple thing, Meredith crept back into the comfort of the warm bed and, at last, fell into a dream-filled sleep.

2

Meredith struggled up through layers of sleep, longing for consciousness, desperately wanting to free herself from the terror of being pursued through the darkness by something unknown, her leaden legs unable to move quickly enough.

With a gasp, she sat up in bed.

It was morning, but clearly not a normal working-day. Cheery yellow walls reflected the sunlight. Disorientated, it took a long minute for her to remember where she was and what she was doing there.

She shook her head free of the nightmare, but not of the noise that accompanied it. Had the dream become reality? There was nothing dreamlike about the thundering hooves. She'd watched enough Westerns to recognise that sound.

Meredith ran to the window. The view from this side of the house was the same as yesterday, green fields and the gentle foothills. The morning dew glistened on the undisturbed pasture.

The rumbling continued, punctuated by loud shouts above the roar of an engine being driven hard in low gear. Hastily, Meredith threw on a tracksuit and trainers and hurried through the house on to the front veranda.

It seemed as if an amateur percussion band was practising just beyond the garden, hidden from her view by bushes.

'If this is the peaceful countryside, then save me from it,' she muttered as she opened the gate and stepped out, ready to have her say.

It was the wrong moment. In a rush of air, a mob of huge, snorting cattle lumbered by her, so close she could hear their rasping breaths and smell their sweating bodies.

She screamed and threw up her arms. The startled cattle veered wildly away from the garden fence and thundered on. A small truck followed, driven recklessly by a madman, his body half out the window, one hand slapping hard on the door panel.

'Get out of the way,' he shouted above the din, increasing the frenzy of his drumming as the truck passed her and bounced alarmingly over the rough terrain in pursuit.

The animals had seen the opening in the fence and beyond it, the road. They charged through to freedom.

Still dazed by her rude awakening, Meredith watched as the man gave up the chase. He got out and rehung the collection of sticks and wire that was the gate, then drove slowly back toward her.

It was only when he stepped from the truck and confronted her that she noticed he was bearded and the beard could not hide his anger. His whole body spoke of it.

'What the devil do you mean by leaving the gate open?' he demanded without introduction.

For a moment she was intimidated, then, working on the theory that attack is the best form of defence, she asked him a question. 'How was I to know that was a gate?'

'You unlocked it to come in, didn't you?'

Meredith had to admit she did. 'To my sorrow,' remembering the disaster and her ruined shoes.

'Then why wouldn't you close it?'

'You don't mean I have to unlock that heap of sticks and wire you call a gate every time I come in and out?'

'Certainly. It's a rule in the country to leave everything as you find it. Open, you leave it open, closed, close it. Every fool knows that.'

She bridled at his labelling her, she didn't like being called a fool. 'And who are you to tell me what to do?'

The man checked at that, as if he realised his rudeness, but when he spoke the anger had not left his voice. 'There are two cottages on Mile End. I live in the other.' He waved an arm towards the hills behind him. 'I'm trying to establish olive tree lots as windbreaks and your carelessness could have wiped them out.'

Meredith refused to look in the direction he indicated. 'The question is, was there any damage done?' she asked belligerently.

'No, but there could have been if they were in the paddock all night.'

Meredith wasn't of a mind to admit grazing cattle might have been one of the disturbing noises that kept her sleepless during the night. There was probably a country rule that required she should get up and chase them away. In the dark.

'As for that so-called gate, I don't intend to drag it back and forth. I'll see Robert Hurst today and have it replaced with something more appropriate. I'm paying enough rent to expect it.'

Having delivered what she considered was the last word on the matter, Meredith turned toward the house, her head held high, eyes straight ahead, her mind already planning what to say to her landlord.

Without warning, her feet encountered a slippery mass and slid from under her. Wildly, her hands searched the empty air for something to break her fall. There was nothing, no-one. She went down, landing heavily on her behind. A warm wetness seeped through her tracksuit pants.

Horrified, she scrambled up, ignoring the outstretched hand that had come too late. She stalked off with as much dignity as she could muster, determined not to look at her neighbour, not wanting him to see how repelled she was by the feel and smell of cattle dung. She suspected that once his anger dissipated he might be laughing at her predicament.

★ ★ ★

In the privacy of the laundry room she shuddered herself out of the soiled

27

clothes and pattered through to the bathroom. It took her ten minutes under the shower and all the hot water to restore her equilibrium.

Enveloped in a cloud of her favourite perfume she retreated to the sunniest corner of the big kitchen. Clasping her coffee mug with both hands, she gazed out on the peaceful scene.

It wasn't the best start to her stay in the country. She had to ask herself if coming here was a mistake? How could she adjust to this way of life? And to the men of the district? Her neighbour, ranting and raving one minute and laughing at her mishap the next.

Meredith wondered about her neighbour. Where was his house? She peered out the window but could see nothing but a disappearing road and bush. He talked of growing olive trees. Where were they? She quashed the twinge of guilt. How was she to know the rules for gates? Or that there would be wandering cows? She thought they all stayed on their own farms.

She realised his anger was all she remembered of him. And his beard. She couldn't say whether he was young or old, only that he was angry. It mattered little, she wouldn't be meeting him again, not once she settled into writing.

The truck was going past her house again, heading for the gate, quietly now, without all the shouting and drumming. She caught a glimpse of the figure of a child beside the driver.

So he was a family man, a bearded family man. She hoped they saw a less angry side to him, he had been quite fierce, looming over her in his rage.

Meredith was still bristling with indignation as she drove the short distance to the township in search of Robert Hurst. There was no-one in the front section of the hardware store, not even an assistant. She marched through the shelves of merchandise to the office. It was deserted, too.

'If you're looking for Rob, he's over on the set.' A bearded old man had come in from the yard. Meredith stared at him. What was it with the beards? She asked herself. Wasn't there a men's hairdresser in town?

'The set?'

'Yes, yes,' the old man replied impatiently, as if she should know. He stumped to the shop window and waved an arm in the direction of the street.

It was turning out to be a day of bad-tempered men. Meredith risked his wrath to repeat her question. 'The set?'

Comprehension lit the weathered face. 'Oh, you don't know about the film they're making here?' He chuckled. 'Reckon you must be the only person in the district who doesn't.'

Meredith was dismayed. Movie-making and hordes of sightseeing fans wasn't her idea of a peaceful rural retreat. Why hadn't Robert Hurst warned her? He must have had plenty of notice, judging by the length of the beards.

'I only arrived yesterday. I've rented Mile End,' she explained, a little stiffly.

'And lucky you are to get it, what with all the tourists that'll be coming.'

'Tourists?'

'Yeah, coming to see the stars while they're making the film. It's about Mad Dog, the bushranger.' He fingered his white beard. 'It's an old-time film,' he explained, in case she didn't know her early Australian history. 'He lived around these parts. Used to hold up the stagecoaches and rob the rich.'

The making of a film wasn't much of a novelty for a city person such as herself, parts of the Central Business District were often closed off to allow filming. But Meredith could imagine that for this little community it was, and it did explain why the three men she'd met so far hadn't shaved for months.

She smiled at the old man and changed the subject. 'The reason for my wanting to see Robert Hurst is that the property needs a new gate.'

'Well, here he is coming now. It's coffee time and he don't like anyone else's coffee but his own.'

Meredith wasn't surprised at that. She had evidence of his good taste in coffee yesterday when she arrived. Had she sub-consciously timed this visit for the morning break?

As she looked out, the tall, hatless figure left a group of men on the other side of the road and strode toward the hardware store. His authoritative air was unchanged but there was an easy swing to his body that she hadn't noticed the day before.

Beyond him, Meredith could see an old-time stagecoach, its shafts as yet empty of horses. Teams of workmen swarmed over the row of shopfronts removing any signs of modernity. She smiled at that — they were so few it was clear why the township had been chosen as a film location.

Stepping inside, Robert Hurst returned her smile. 'It's good to get a cheerful greeting,' he remarked.

She turned from the scene with a puzzled face. 'Sorry?'

'This morning isn't going so well. Everyone is complaining about something.'

'Oh.' For a moment she considered sparing him any more aggravation, then wondered why she should. His day wasn't her worry, he was only her landlord.

'Mr Hurst — '

'Please call me Rob, everyone does.'

His manner was quite charming, but the thought of the contraption he considered was a gate and the part it played in her day hardened her resolve. She wondered should she ask for compensation for her ruined clothes.

'Mr Hurst, surely you don't consider that mess of wire and sticks at the entrance to Mile End a gate, do you?'

'Rob,' he corrected her. 'So you are complaining, too. You disappoint me.' She didn't believe him. It was doubtful anything about her would affect him. He waved in the direction of his office. 'Come in and sit down.'

Meredith's eyes went immediately to

the cupboard that hid the coffee machine. He didn't take the hint, choosing instead to sit in the comfortable chair behind his desk.

'Now, I've heard you had trouble this morning.'

She didn't want to ask how he knew about that. 'Trouble?' she asked sarcastically. 'Not really, unless you call being frightened out of my wits by cattle, stepping in fresh cow manure and being insulted by a stranger, to be trouble. All because of that so-called gate. Why haven't you got something better than that?'

The man behind the desk said nothing, intent on ratting among the papers before him. Meredith's fingers itched to organise his filing system. At last he produced an order form and passed it across to her.

'As you can see by the invoice, one has already been ordered. However, priority is being given to work connected with the making of the film. The manufacturers figure that benefits the whole town, not just one or two. So we'll have to be patient and manage as best we can, won't we?'

It was hard to argue with such a reasonable man without appearing shrewish. There was still the possibility of being offered coffee to consider.

Although he must've known what she was thinking he moved on smoothly. 'Would you like to look over the film set?' he asked.

She didn't hesitate. 'Thank you, but no,' she replied, shaking her head. 'I have shopping to do before going back to Mile End. After all, I am here to work.'

Her refusal didn't seem to offend him. In fact, nothing seemed to ruffle his manner toward her. For some reason this annoyed Meredith.

'And what work would that be?' he asked.

She looked at him sharply, ready to take offence at the slightest sign of being patronised, but there was none. He appeared genuinely interested, in a polite sort of way.

'I've taken three months off work to come and live in the country so that I can write a novel,' she said, almost daring him to laugh at her dream.

He didn't.

'In peace and quiet,' she added, thinking how the rude awakening that morning had been just the opposite. He began laughing then, provoking her question. 'How did you know about that?'

'Josh, your neighbour, came by with the very same enquiry as you. He wanted to know when the gate was being installed.'

'Then perhaps he told you I ruined a perfectly good outfit, and expensive shoes.'

Rob Hurst curbed his amusement. 'I'm sorry to hear that. Perhaps you should consider more suitable footwear out here in the country,' he suggested, glancing at her shoes. 'We carry a line of good walking boots that might do the job.'

She knew he was right — her shoes were too light for non-city walking, and that would include this township with its rough pavements. But great clunking boots weren't her idea of smart dressing. And for some reason, the thought of Rob Hurst fitting her with shoes unsettled her.

She looked about her for an excuse. The old man was pottering about out of hearing.

'You must be busy,' she said. 'Perhaps your assistant could help me.'

He laughed heartily. 'If you are thinking of renovating or gardening, Joe's your man, but boots, no. And he'd be the first to admit it.' Still smiling at the thought, he turned to the cupboard that housed the coffee machine.

Behind his back, Meredith tried to hide her anticipation.

'You've time for a coffee?' he asked, half-turning his head.

She hesitated a moment too long.

'Give you strength,' he teased. 'For the boot-buying exercise.'

A sudden thought crossed her mind. If he was so good at gauging her reaction to everything, was he aware of how much it annoyed her? That meant he was doing it deliberately. She had to ask herself why.

Determined to act as nonchalantly as him, she put on a bland face. 'I haven't decided on the boots,' she demurred.

'But you will,' he said. 'You know I'm right.'

That was the trouble. From the moment their paths crossed it was as if there was some kind of city-versus-country competition and he was coming out in front.

Meredith didn't like that at all.

3

Meredith sat staring at the blank computer screen. It had been that way for what seemed like hours. No matter how hard she tried, the longed-for flow of words would not come.

She heard the faint click of the garden gate catch, and the light steps skipping along the gravel path to the side of the house. The figure of a child blocked the light.

'Why, hello!' Meredith exclaimed, glad of the interruption. She rose from her chair and opened the fly-wire screen.

Her visitor was a tousled-haired girl, about six years old. Under clean but faded denim overalls she wore a bright blue T-shirt that matched her eyes. A canvas sun-hat tied under her chin had been pushed back off her head and rested atop the junior-size back-pack.

'I'm Cassie,' she announced, stepping

into the room with a self-possessed air.

'My name is Meredith.'

'Yes, I know.' The computer was like a magnet to the child. 'What are you doing?'

'I'm writing. No. I'm trying to write a story.'

'Oh, I like writing stories. Uncle Josh says I'm good.'

Meredith tried to hide her smile. 'It must help to have encouragement.'

'Yes, and he knows what's a good story because he's a school-teacher.'

'I suppose that makes sense,' Meredith agreed. 'Do you go to his school?'

'Of course,' the child replied matter-of-factly, as if that was a silly question and didn't need elaboration. She was more interested in the computer.

'A work in progress, chapter one,' she slowly read aloud from the blue screen. 'What does that mean?'

'It's the heading for the story I'm going to write. I haven't thought up a title yet.' Nor anything else, Meredith mused. Who could have imagined it would be so difficult? The authors she dealt with spoke glibly of thousands of words a day, yet here she was, unable to put down one line. Perhaps getting started was hard for every writer, but wasn't admitted.

'That's not the way to start a story!' Cassie said.

'It's not?'

Somehow the slight figure had wriggled her way into Meredith's chair, legs dangling well short of the floor, her face earnest as her little fingers picked out the letters to write, *once upon a time*.

She looked up. 'That's the proper way to write a story,' she said, authoritatively. 'Every story begins with once upon a time.'

Meredith was impressed by the logic. 'Of course. Where else? Thank you, that will be a great help. Now, would you like a glass of milk and perhaps a piece of bun?'

The child slithered eagerly off the chair and followed Meredith to the kitchen.

'I hope you like buns, Cassie. This

one's fresh today,' Meredith said as she buttered a slice.

'You could toast it if it's not. That's okay with me. Uncle Josh often does. That way there's nothing wasted.'

'A very good idea.'

'Uncle Josh has lots of good ideas.'

Meredith turned away to the refrigerator to hide another smile. 'A glass of milk?' she asked, returning to the table with the jug. 'Tell me, why aren't you at school?'

'I've been today.' The comment was delivered with a note of exasperation, as if Meredith should understand the daily routine of a country school.

Corrected on that point, Meredith wondered how she could satisfy her curiosity as to where the child had come from. It seemed her Uncle Josh was the bearded man who had bellowed about the gate and then laughed at her predicament as she slipped in the cattle manure? Perhaps there was an extended family in the hidden house with the olive trees.

'Did you walk over from your house?'

'Oh, no, that's too far.' A fine moustache of milk adorned Cassie's upper lip, reminding Meredith she hadn't supplied her guest with a napkin. 'No, Uncle Josh brought me.'

'He dropped you off here?' Meredith was astonished. The nerve of the man! Insult her one minute and expect her to baby-sit the next.

Cassie didn't seem to regard the supplying of further information as urgent. She chewed carefully until her mouth was empty before answering. 'He brought me with him and I got bored and walked down to see you.'

Meredith wondered if she had the patience to wait for this well-brought up child to fill in the details of her day without having to resort to interrogation.

'There's a lot I don't know,' she confided. 'Perhaps you could put me in the picture.'

This seemed to be the right thing to say. Cassie drank the last of the milk, and ran her tongue around her mouth. 'What is it you want to know?' she asked in a business-like way.

Meredith laughed at herself. The child had seen through her subterfuge. 'We could start with you telling me where Uncle Josh is now.'

'He's at the gate, of course.'

'Of course. But what is he doing there?'

'He's putting up a new gate so that the cattle — '

'A new gate?' Meredith pushed back her chair and hurried out of the room, down the hall and out on to the veranda. To her disappointment, it wasn't possible to see very far because of the garden trees.

She returned to the kitchen, and her visitor. 'I'm sorry to leave you like that, Cassie, but I was so excited. A new gate means I won't get tangled up in the old one any more.' It also meant I got through to the cool Robert Hurst, she exulted. And caught him out.

Cassie got down from the table.

'That's all right,' she said. 'I have to be going anyway. I told Uncle Josh I wouldn't be long. He knew it was boring for me, watching him dig a hole for a post.'

They walked to the garden gate together. 'I'm so pleased you got bored and came to see me,' Meredith smiled. 'I hope you'll come again.'

'Not if you're writing stories, I won't. Uncle Josh wouldn't like that.'

It seemed to Meredith that Uncle Josh had a lot to say. She decided perhaps it was time she checked him out. Her writing could begin in earnest tomorrow.

'Would you like me to run you down to the gate in my car?'

Before Cassie could come up with one of Uncle Josh's homilies, she went on, 'It wouldn't be a trouble and I would like to see the new gate if I'm to use it.'

The girl looked down the long driveway toward the entrance to the property then back to Meredith.

'If you're sure you won't be bored, too,' she said, for the first time showing the beginnings of doubt.

Thoroughly captivated by her visitor, Meredith took Cassie's hand. 'I can assure you I'll be most interested,' she said and led the way to the car.

★   ★   ★

As they drove up to the gate, Meredith recognised the truck as the one that has chased the cattle past her cottage earlier that day. And standing beside it, its bearded driver.

Cassie was out of the car in double quick time and raced to greet the man, throwing herself against his legs. Meredith followed more slowly, carefully picking her way through the evidence of the early morning intruders.

'Uncle Josh, look who brought me back. It saved me from getting tired,' Cassie cried.

From the impression she formed during their first encounter, Meredith expected the man's response to the child to be impatient or even short-tempered. It wasn't. There was nothing of the angry man about him as he put an arm out to hold his niece close to him.

'What a win for you, Possum,' he said, gazing down at her fondly.

Meredith stood watching this display of obvious affection, ignored by the bearded Josh as he gave the child his complete attention.

Cassie had more to tell. 'And do you know what, Meredith is writing stories, too. Just like me.'

At last, Cassie's uncle acknowledged Meredith's presence. He turned to her, his face still soft with affection for the child. He said nothing. Vivid blue eyes outlined by thick, sooty lashes took in every detail of her appearance.

Meredith stared back. The man was quite tall, and well-built. A battered bush-hat covered his head and the exposed sun-tanned shoulders hinted at an outdoor life. Rather surprising for a schoolteacher, she thought. As with Rob Hurst, the dark beard disguised the contours of his face.

'You're a writer?' he asked at last. He didn't seem over impressed and she wondered did she imagine a sneer? Something didn't please him.

She stepped forward with hand outstretched to introduce herself. 'Meredith Gale,' she said, raising her eyebrows in anticipation of him returning the gesture.

He didn't. Instead he walked to the truck and began dragging a shining new gate along its tray.

'Could you give me a hand?'

Meredith stood astonished. 'You expect me to help lift that?'

'Yes, just take one end. It would make it easier for me.'

It smacked of bad organisation and she couldn't help being critical. 'Why didn't you think of getting help before you brought it out here?'

'Everyone in town is busy.'

Meredith knew that to be true. Rob

Hurst had explained priority was being given to the film production company.

'Keeping wandering cattle out is important to me, and as I can't rely on you to keep the old gate closed, I decided to hurry up delivery by going to the factory myself.'

'Wasn't this a school day? Aren't you the teacher?' she asked, not wanting to admit to her shortcomings where country ways were concerned.

'I called off lessons for this afternoon.' He stopped dragging the gate and balanced the overhang on his hip. 'Look, I could manage on my own, but it seems to me it's a small thing for you to do.'

'A small thing? That's a wide gate.'

'Of course, it has to be wide enough for trucks.'

That made Meredith mad.

'I know that,' she said. 'What I mean is . . . ' She didn't know what she meant. The whole idea was so ridiculous. She hadn't come to the country to help install gates, she had come to write a novel and this didn't get it started.

'I'll help you, Uncle Josh,' Cassie offered.

'Thank you, Cassie,' replied her uncle. 'You can look after the nuts and bolts until I'm ready to use them. They're in a box on the front seat in the truck.'

Meredith knew the child hadn't meant to make her feel guilty but now she did — no-one else had left the gate open and this was pay-back time.

There was no visible change of expression on the man's face, but he must have been aware it was a point scored.

She looked down helplessly at her leisure-suit. It was her favourite. Perhaps if she was careful she wouldn't have to ruin this one.

'You'll take this end and I'll take the full weight as it comes off the truck,' he persisted.

Meredith wasn't going to give in to his demands without a show of independence.

'I think it would be polite of you to

introduce yourself,' she said with reasonable sweetness, quite aware that standing holding the gate must be tiring for him. His straining biceps told her that.

To her surprise he answered as if he knew what her game was and didn't intend to give her satisfaction with an ill-tempered retort. 'I'm Josh Logan,' he replied.

'Cassie's uncle?' she asked, delaying his relief a little longer.

'Yes,' he said, a little shortly, she thought. 'Come over here and take my place.'

It was no longer a game. 'But that's heavy,' she protested.

'You won't have to bear all the weight,' he explained. 'I'll be taking most of it as I pull it further off the truck.'

Meredith hesitated, looking at her manicured nails and wondering how to help him and protect them, and her clothes, at the same time.

He lost patience at last. 'Just grab it,'

he ordered in what she imagined was his schoolteacher voice.

Meredith surprised herself by doing as she was told, taking hold of the iron frame as he moved it off the truck. The transferred weight caught her unawares. She grunted and almost buckled at the knees, only her pride keeping her upright.

Afterwards, she wondered why she bothered. Intent on what he was doing and taking no notice of her, Josh Logan moved quickly towards the new gate-post.

Indignation rose in her. Who did this country schoolteacher think he was? She had no choice but to totter after him or lose her grip and risk his wrath.

Suddenly, the weight was taken off her completely as the gate slotted into place on the prepared hinges.

She realised her hands were stinging and held them up for examination. Red welts stood out across both palms.

Dismayed, she turned them over. Despite her care, several of her fingernails had been broken. Where would she get a manicure? It was hardly likely the little township would boast such a service.

'Well, if that's all you need me for, I'll . . . ' Meredith said rather stiffly.

Josh Logan turned his head in her direction. 'Er, yes, thank you.'

'I'm helping,' Cassie said unnecessarily, not moving from his side.

Meredith wasn't used to being ignored. Where she came from her services were valued. Fuming, and without a backward glance, she marched to her car and, in a spurt of gravel, drove it away.

4

The next morning the new gate swung wide on its hinges at the touch of Meredith's hand. Although he was lacking in manners, she had to give Josh Logan credit for knowing how to hang a gate, and for getting the job done. But it had come at a cost to her.

Her nails were ruined. That meant another trip into the township, this time for a manicure.

Like every business in the little township, the Warrawilla beauty salon was affected by the arrival of the film crew, Chloe, the owner explained, and was fully booked. Meredith hadn't understood that.

'Don't the film company bring their own hairdressers and make-up people?' she asked.

'Yes, but everyone in the district wants to look their best,' Chloe confided over the phone. 'The extras for the film haven't been chosen yet and no-one knows if the talent scouts are about on the streets or not. They could be.'

Modern hairstyles won't help their cause if it's an historical film, Meredith thought grumpily, but didn't say so.

She smiled at the thought of Cassie and wondered were all six year olds as engaging. She wouldn't know. Children hardly featured in her world of thirty-something and single-in-the-city.

'I would appreciate a manicure if you could possibly make room for me.' She juggled the phone between her ear and shoulder and examined her broken nails. 'I need a repair job.'

The hairdresser hummed and then found a solution. 'I'll ask Bev to come in especially. She helps out when I'm busy at Christmas. I suppose you could say all our Christmases have come at once.' She gave a giggle, then became more business-like. 'There may be a surcharge — '

'I'll be happy to pay it,' Meredith cut in quickly. A wicked thought crossed her mind. She could send the bill to Josh Logan, after all, he was responsible.

The main street was empty. Meredith was able to park right in front of the hardware shop. Was it lunchtime or just her good luck?

She checked her watch and decided there was one advantage to country living — the parking. She locked the car and crossed the pavement to keep her appointment next door.

The hairdresser wasn't at all as Meredith had imagined her from their telephone conversation. The exotic name and young voice materialised into a dumpy, middle-aged woman, whose conventional hair style was no advertisement for the salon. Meredith hoped she would be good with the scissors when the time came for a trim.

Bev, the manicurist, a replica of Chloe, clucked over Meredith's hands.

'Goodness, what have you been

doing? We'll have to start all over, I'm afraid. It'll cost,' she warned, naming a price.

Meredith hid her surprise. Even Josh Logan would be able to afford this. The forces of supply and demand obviously hadn't made inroads into the world of beauty in Warrawilla.

'You're a stranger around here?' Chloe enquired over the wet head of her client. Meredith would have thought that was obvious. No doubt the hairdresser knew everyone and everything and probably was honour-bound to keep the women of the community fully informed about any newcomers.

'I've leased Mile End for three months.'

Chloe anchored the last roller with a plastic pin and reached up for the overhead hairdryer. 'Are you connected with the film people?'

'No.' Meredith became aware of three sets of eyes turned in her direction and realised more was required of her.

'I'm a writer.' She felt a twinge of

guilt at that. It was more like a would-be writer or, as her friends would say, a wannabe-writer. She hadn't actually written a sentence, and Cassie's opening words mocked her. Once Upon A Time, indeed! That was the trouble, there hadn't been time.

The eyes of the three women were round with alarm but it was left to Chloe to voice their concern. 'We're not going to be in a book, are we?'

Meredith hastened to allay their fears. 'Oh, no, it's going to be about city people.' The only people I really know, she admitted to herself.

Satisfied, Chloe continued with the questioning. 'Are you on your own then?' she asked, nudging the client's head under the dryer and switching it on.

Meredith thought of her regular salon in the city. After years of patronage it was like a second home, the staff, and the drama of their daily lives, the nearest thing to family she knew.

She recognised the country friendliness of these women, but it would take time to build up that kind of a rapport. But she had to begin somewhere. 'Yes, I'm single. Do you have a family?'

Chloe didn't need much encouragement to talk about her domestic arrangements as she bustled around the salon preparing for the next client. The manicure had reached the stage where Meredith had one hand free. Chloe brought a mug of instant coffee and placed it within easy reach. Meredith sighed and thought of Rob Hurst in the hardware shop next door. And his coffee-making machine. She could almost smell the brew.

Another hairdressing client had arrived. She brought with her a clutch of grandchildren — and the reason for the quietness of the street.

'Yes, they're starting filming today, taking background shots of the main street. My Tom is supplying the horses for the stagecoach, as you know, Chloe, and of course, he had to drive them.'

'Won't have to dress up, then, will he?' Bev teased. 'Just wear his everyday clothes, eh?'

The three women laughed good-naturedly. 'Tom's no fashion plate,' his wife admitted. 'Doesn't throw out clothes that are still good. He says they don't make things like they used to.'

There was general agreement between the women, before the older one went on. 'His parents were the same. I've got boxes of their clothes. The wardrobe mistress is very interested. And one thing is certain, it's going to be hard getting Tom to shave when all this is over. He fancies himself in a beard.' She looked to see if the children were taking any notice, and lowered her voice. 'I do, too. Very sexy.'

There was another laugh all round and a commotion at the door.

'Like this one,' Chloe said, behind her hand.

Meredith had to agree with her. Rob Hurst's maleness, reflected in the mirrors, seemed to fill the cluttered salon.

He carefully stepped over the children and their colouring books. 'Your car,' he growled down at her without a greeting. 'You'll have to shift it out of the way.'

She was almost pleased to see him ruffled. It proved he wasn't perfect. 'Sorry?'

'Didn't you see the *No Parking* signs?' he demanded.

'No parking? In Warrawilla?'

'Were there any other vehicles parked in the street?'

Meredith had to admit there hadn't been. 'I thought I was lucky to have picked a quiet morning,'

'A quiet morning!' Rob Hurst exploded.

'Having a bad day?' she teased, mainly for the women's benefit, not in the least intimidated by the man.

He didn't seem pleased by her attitude but made an effort to control his irritation. 'As these ladies could have told you, the film company began filming opening scenes of the street this morning. Blind Freddy could see something was up.'

Meredith had to admit he had a point. Intent on the need to have her nails repaired, she hadn't taken notice of her surroundings.

The absence of vehicles and, now that she thought of it, the tarmac covered by a thick layer of sand, should have been enough for her to put two and two together. Even with the salon talk about filming she hadn't made the connection between the activities and her car.

'I'll have to ask you to move it.'

'Move it?' She looked down at her hands, then at the dismay of Bev's face.

'She can't leave now, her nails aren't dry,' exclaimed Bev and Chloe at the same time. The children, sensing trouble, looked up.

'Well, give me the keys,' he suggested in a more reasonable tone. 'I'll do it.'

'I can't, my nails.'

Meredith looked at her handbag on the bench in front of her. For a second she hesitated, wondering was there anything personal in it that she wouldn't want him to see. She decided money, keys, a mobile telephone and cosmetics wouldn't fuel male derision as to what women kept in their bags.

It would be different if she was carrying her everyday work bag. That usually contained everything for a full-scale emergency.

She nodded the go-ahead.

'Where will I find it?' she called to his departing back, but he showed no sign of hearing her.

'I think he fancies you,' Chloe suggested slyly.

Meredith was more worried about her keys. 'How will I get into my car?'

'He'll leave them in the ignition.'

'Leave the keys in the ignition?' she squealed, all her city anxieties activated.

'Keep still,' Bev ordered, taking a tighter grip on Meredith's hand as she applied the last coat of nail polish. 'Don't worry, no-one locks their car around here. Who would steal it, anyway?'

Meredith had an answer for that. 'There must be a lot of strangers about at present.'

'True,' Chloe agreed, giving her a significant look. 'But they don't stay strangers for long, do they?'

Meredith laughed at that. 'Touche!' she said.

The little encounter with Rob Hurst had bonded them. Together, they watched through the window as he reversed her car from the kerb and disappeared down a side street.

'Mmmm, very sexy,' Chloe mused, getting back to her job. 'Pity we're married, eh, girls?'

'And too old for him,' added the grandmother.

Meredith felt all eyes on her.

'Some of us aren't,' Chloe said. 'As I said, he fancies you, Meredith.' She put down her comb and scissors and carefully removed the cape from her client's shoulders. The finished cut was stylish, Meredith was pleased to note, thinking of the future and ignoring

Chloe's remarks. They had become quite friendly but not enough, she didn't think, to discuss her romantic life like this.

Deliberately avoiding Chloe's knowing grin, she paid Bev for the manicure.

'Now, where will I find my car?'

'He'll have parked it in the lane behind the shop,' Chloe said. 'Come out this way,' she said, opening a back door.

There was a sudden exodus of the grandmother and the children. Meredith followed, and found herself in a narrow back lane. The car had been backed in the keys left in the ignition. Despite Chloe's insistence it was safe, she hadn't been easy about that.

A piece of paper, obviously torn from a notebook, lay on the driver's seat. Was this Warrawilla's version of a parking ticket? She picked it up.

Meredith, the note read, *I'm having a dinner for the production crew tonight. Would you like to come? I'll call you.*

The writing was clear and bold, but

the signature was an unreadable scribble. She presumed it was from Rob Hurst. He was the only one who knew where her car was parked.

So Chloe was right. As she so quaintly put it, he fancied her, despite his impatience over her parking. He must do. Why else would he invite her? They had no business dealings or anything like that to discuss.

She wasn't sure how she felt about him. He certainly was attractive, but then, there'd never been a shortage of good-looking guys in her life. This one would be no different. Except for the beard! She wondered what kissing a man with a bushy beard was like.

Spreading her fingers out from the steering-wheel, she admired her manicure before starting the car. At the end of the lane she swung to the left. Along with her nails, her good humour had been restored. There was nothing to keep her in the township, she would be able to get on with her writing at last.

Until Rob Hurst's phone call came

66

and she had to decide what to wear to a dinner in the country. Nothing too sophisticated, she wouldn't think, if Chloe and Bev's work outfits were anything to go by.

* * *

Parking in front of the hardware store was out of the question that evening. A row of cars had already taken up all the spaces. Meredith crossed from the opposite side of the dimly-lit street and began to climb the ornamental cast-iron staircase that clung to the outside of the old building.

It wasn't easy, several times she had to grab at the side rail when a heel of her strappy sandals became caught in the fretwork and she stumbled. After one particularly wild lurch she wondered had she done any permanent damage.

Suddenly, a welcome flood of light made the job easier. She looked up to see Rob standing in the open doorway.

Behind him, she glimpsed a roomful of other guests.

'Thank goodness,' Meredith gasped. 'How did you know I was here?'

'Light sensors,' he replied briefly. She couldn't tell much about his mood from the tone of his voice. 'We take pity on our visitors at the halfway mark.'

She reached him. 'If you really want to take pity on your visitors perhaps you could do something about the steps themselves,' she said, lifting a foot and twisting her head back over her shoulder to examine the sole of her sandal. 'I think I'm in danger of losing a heel.'

He moved farther out on to the landing. 'Here, let me see,' he said, quite pleasantly.

Meredith slipped off the suspect sandal. He took it and brought it down heavily on the handrail. The whole staircase clanged.

'There, all fixed now,' he said, running his fingers over the inner sole before returning it.

He was standing so close it was natural to reach out a hand to his shoulder to balance herself whilst she put the sandal back on her foot.

'Those are hardly the sort of things to wear in the country. Remember, I did try to sell you something more suitable.'

So much for Chloe's suggestion that he fancied her. Nothing she did was right. She straightened up quickly, taking her hand away.

'Boots? For a dinner party?' The idea made her snort. And gave her courage to speak her mind. 'I don't know why you feel you have to point-score by criticising me and everything I do.'

He looked astonished. 'Criticise you? How do you mean? I'm just trying to help you, as a newcomer to the district.'

She wondered could she really believe what he was saying. It was hard to tell. He put a friendly arm around her shoulder and steered her toward the door. 'Come on in and meet everyone.'

The first thing Meredith noticed was

the sprinkling of clean-shaven men in the crowded room. She decided they must be the guests of honour, the production team.

'Here's someone you know, my neighbour. She'll look after you whilst I get you a drink. Now, what will you have?'

Meredith could hardly contain her surprise. Chloe in party gear was a different person to Chloe, the hairdresser. The little black dress did wonders for her figure, and the conventional hairstyle had been blow-waved into a fly-away style.

'A white wine, please,' Meredith answered.

Chloe was triumphant. 'There, I told you Rob fancied you!' she crowed as soon as he left them.

'What makes you think that?' Meredith asked, wondering why Chloe showed no surprise at seeing her. She couldn't have known about the scribbled invitation in her car.

'I'm not just a pretty face. He's been

watching the door like a hawk.'

And obviously, so have you, thought Meredith. Determined not to give the idea any encouragement, she played dumb. 'So?'

'Well, there are no other young single women here tonight, and he wouldn't be excited about any of us locals.'

Meredith looked around the room again. She'd been so taken by the number of beardless men she hadn't noticed the other guests. Chloe was right. All the women were much older than her.

And more casually dressed in trousers. And wearing boots, she noticed. Was she the only one who didn't know about the staircase? The increasingly familiar feeling of being an outsider swept over her.

Her host was back with a glass of white wine. 'What say you and I declare a truce?'

Chloe raised her eyebrows suggestively, wiggled her fingers in a goodbye gesture and moved away.

'Whatever do you mean?' Meredith asked, stalling for time. She had to be careful how she answered.

He was right, there had been tension between them from the very first. On her part it had been because he treated her so casually, she wasn't used to that. She sipped at her wine, and looked at him.

Was Chloe right? She couldn't see any signs of him fancying her, as the hairdresser put it. He was less harassed now than he'd been over her car, but as to that being considered showing an interest in her, well!

'I mean your city-versus-country attitude.'

'Oh,' she said, glad she hadn't rushed in with a comment — she would have gotten it wrong.

'You must admit we don't do things the way you city folk do. For one thing, we're more laid-back.'

Meredith felt she should defend herself. 'I'm used to a . . . rather hectic lifestyle.'

Something about him changed, she couldn't be sure what. 'Well, I'd better liven things up for you and introduce you to the other guests, starting with your neighbour, Josh Logan.'

'That should certainly liven things up,' she murmured.

'Oh, yes, I forgot. You've already met, haven't you?' He was steering her around little knots of people. 'Let's see if we can mend fences.'

'Fences? I don't think that's a good choice of words,' she laughed rather nervously.

He was still chuckling when they came upon Josh Logan standing quietly on the edge of an earnest group of locals.

'Josh!'

Cassie's uncle turned at the greeting. Meredith caught her breath. Dressed for the occasion, the man was quite handsome. His dark curly hair, no longer hidden by his bush-hat, had been allowed to grow, too, and curled over his collar. She had forgotten how remarkable his eyes were. She saw a flash of teeth as they recognised his host and he put out a hand.

'Rob!'

'Have your formally met your neighbour?' Rob asked, with a glimmer of a smile.

The vivid eyes turned on her. And became cool. 'Yes, we've met,' Josh responded.

Meredith felt the snub. Whatever was with the man? Surely the business of the straying cattle was over and done with or did he expect a solicitor's letter of apology? She decided to let it go over her head.

'Yes, Rob, we've met and I also met his delightful niece, Cassie.' She looked into his eyes, daring him to be unpleasant. 'How is she, Josh? I hope she'll come and visit me again soon.'

He returned her gaze. 'I think not,' he said.

5

Thinking about it afterwards, Meredith could find several perfectly good reasons to justify her behaviour. She was thrown off balance by this new environment, that was one.

These two men had wrong-footed her and sapped her confidence, that was another. And the frustration at not being able to begin writing her novel, yet another. All good reasons.

But for the moment, she didn't rationalise her actions. She just knew he'd rebuffed her and she didn't need the aggravation. Angrily, she turned away and, without a word to either man, made for the door.

The room was not large, and making a quick exit shouldn't have been a problem. But other guests and pieces of furniture seemed to be in her way. By the time she'd excused herself through the crowd and reached the door, Rob was already there, waiting for her. He put out an arm to block her way.

'Hey! Where are you going?'

'If you people think insulting me will send me back to the city in a hissy-fit, you're wrong. I came here for a reason, and I'm going to stay for that reason. But I want nothing to do with you all.'

He leaned forward and opened the door, shepherding her out on to the landing, and closing it behind them. 'Now, what's this about?'

'That Josh Logan! I've apologised about the gate and the straying cattle, but he's not going to let me forget it.'

Rob looked puzzled. 'I didn't hear him mention the gate or the cattle.'

'No, he didn't say that but it's what he's doing, not letting Cassie come to visit!' Meredith replied, indignation lifting her voice to a higher pitch.

His beard hid any smile that might be on his face but Meredith could tell he wasn't taking her seriously. Just like men, sticking together, ganging up on her. The sooner she got down the stairs and into her car the better. She tossed her head and tried to step past him.

'Whoa! You're not going anywhere until I've sorted this out. Come back inside.'

'Frankly, I don't want — '

The door swung open behind them and a woman's voice called, 'Rob! The food's ready!'

His arm snaked across in front of Meredith and caught her shoulder, tightening his grip to turn her away from the stairs.

'At least come and enjoy the meal. You can't go home now and begin cooking. Not in that gorgeous outfit.'

That made her smile in spite of herself. 'Flattery will get you everything.'

*　　*　　*

After Rob had piled her plate with delicious food from the buffet, he introduced her to one of the production crew.

'Meredith, this is Stefan, the director of the film. Stefan, Meredith.'

'Oh, so you're Meredith,' Stefan said in a heavily accented voice. 'If I'd known you were such a good-looker I wouldn't have cursed you to high heaven.'

Meredith was astonished. 'Cursed me?'

'That's a mild exaggeration on my part, I must admit. But I was angry. You spoiled a good shot. We had to go again.'

'I what?'

'You drove your car out from a side street on to the main street and right into the action, horses and all.'

Meredith was dismayed. It wasn't only the locals she was upsetting, now the film people were off-side.

'How was I to know . . . ?' she began, then stopped. She should've known, it was the talk of the hairdressing salon, and Rob had told her when he came to move her car. She'd forgotten all about it. How had that happened? Was she losing her grip? What had driven all thought of the filming out of her head?

The director hadn't heard the beginnings of her attempt to justify herself. 'But, as I say, you're a looker, just what I need, so I'll forgive you,' he went on. 'Have you thought of doing some film work?' he asked, putting out a hand to lift her chin, tilting her face this way and that, peering at her from different angles. Next, he took her empty plate out of her hands and directed her to walk.

Bemused by his charisma, and unable to take offence at the familiarity, Meredith laughed. 'Walk? In this crowded room? You must be joking.'

He wasn't. He tapped his fork against his wine glass to attract attention. 'Listen up, folks,' he called. No-one seemed to mind being interrupted, obediently turning towards him and becoming quiet. 'I want to see Meredith walk, so clear a path.'

There was an authority about the man, he was used to giving orders and having them carried out. Without thinking about it, Meredith obeyed him, too. As the guests parted, she stepped out and walked the length of the room, unafraid of the attention.

It became a bit of fun, the guests clapping rhythmically and stamping their feet. She smiled at an approving Chloe as she passed.

The performance was going well — it was time to execute a model's pirouette and return to Stefan.

Suddenly, her feet missed a beat, the fancy footwork almost became a stumble. Josh Logan was standing at the back of the room, his hands deep in his pockets, his bearded face unreadable. Meredith realised she had forgotten about him until now.

In the brief moment before she turned she recognised his body language said it all — not interested. Not even amused.

She wondered why he was so serious. Family worries, perhaps. Or dislike of her? So what? She could handle that.

Stefan was pleased. 'Good,' he pronounced as she reached him. 'Rob, see this girl is in wardrobe first thing in the morning,' he called before wandering off to refill his glass.

Rob appeared beside her with a bottle and two champagne flutes. 'That performance deserves a toast,' he said, skilfully pouring their drinks and disposing of the bottle on to a nearby table.

'You were smiling. You should do it more often, you have a wonderful smile.' He clinked his glass against hers. 'Here's to the city meeting the country and smiling.'

Meredith couldn't take offence at that, either. He was right, she had been grumpy about everything since she arrived in Warrawilla.

'I'll drink to that,' she said, recklessly gulping the champagne.

The bubbles tickled the back of her nose. 'Why is Josh Logan so serious?' she asked, a little surprised at her question. As if it mattered.

81

Rob seemed momentarily surprised, too. 'Josh?' He moved closer. 'We don't want to talk about him, do we?'

'Congratulations!' Chloe gushed as soon as she got within earshot. 'We'll be working together. I've been booked to help with the hair of the extras.'

'Meredith won't be an extra, Chloe.'

Both women turned their attention to Rob Hurst.

'What do you mean?' Chloe asked him. 'We all heard what Stefan said.'

Meredith answered for herself. 'He's right, I won't be an extra. I have something else I want to do. I'm here to write a novel.'

Rob ignored her reply. 'You won't be an extra, Stefan has picked you out for a role.' He smiled. 'Not a starring one, I admit, but what they call a featured role, maybe a few lines of dialogue and your name in the credits and all that.'

Chloe was even more delighted. She embraced Meredith enthusiastically. 'I'm so pleased for you. When you're a famous film star in Hollywood we can say we knew you.'

Meredith was feeling overwhelmed. It had been a fun thing until now. 'Didn't you hear me? I won't be taking up the offer, if that's what it is.' She turned to Rob. 'I don't understand the part you play in all this. Who are you?'

'He's the producer's representative,' interposed Chloe before he could answer.

'The executive producer is back in Los Angeles and yes, I'm his representative on location. But I'm also the liaison between the townsfolk and the film-makers.'

There were other questions Meredith wanted to ask Rob, but Chloe, still on a high, had her own agenda.

'What will I have to do, Rob?'

'Get up very early on shooting days,' Rob replied in a teasing voice. 'She's a night owl,' he confided to Meredith in a loud whisper.

'Won't that interfere with your salon hours, Chloe?' she asked.

The hairdresser had that all worked out.

'It's not every day and anyway, the extras are locals and my clients.' She excused herself to spread her good news.

'Now, where were we?' Rob asked, moving close to Meredith again. She felt a little uneasy. She wasn't ready for him to become personal.

'We were getting it straight that I am not interested in a role in this film,' she answered in a matter-of-fact voice.

Taking his cue from that, he became business-like. 'The pay is higher than that for an extra.'

Meredith raised her eyebrows. 'So?'

'You don't have to be on the set before sun-up . . . '

'What part of not interested don't you understand?' she asked. Even as she spoke she thought of the double meaning. Would Rob take that to mean she wasn't interested in him as a man? And was that the truth?

Now that a truce had been declared

between them he came across as an attractive personality, despite the beard.

Whatever his interpretation of her remark, the result was what she wanted, he gave up trying to persuade her. 'All right, if you don't want to become an actor, that's OK with me. I'll tell Stefan tomorrow. No need to spoil his party.'

She laughed at that. 'I don't think me refusing his offer could spoil Stefan's party. Look at him.'

The music had changed from a background of pleasant classical to full-on disco and the director was dancing on the hastily-cleared table.

Meredith woke the next morning determined to begin the serious business of writing her novel. It was why she'd come to Warrawilla. Over breakfast she reviewed the notes on the plot she'd made in the city.

It was a good storyline, she knew that, all it needed was work to bring the characters to life.

But when she sat down at the

computer, Cassie's words leapt at her from the screen and she began thinking about the child. And her enigmatic Uncle Josh.

Was he as petty as he seemed? How did leaving a gate open make her an unsuitable companion for his niece? Or was it more than that? Did he have an aversion to people from the city?

She got up and went through to the kitchen window, to gaze in that direction. There was nothing to see but bush. An idea came to her. She would drive over and perhaps meet his wife and find answers to her questions.

Without pausing to close down her computer in case the impulse died, Meredith checked her appearance and hurried to the carport.

★ ★ ★

The gravelled road that went past her cottage soon disappeared into a mini-forest before emerging into a picture-postcard valley. Meredith sighed with pleasure and let the car slow to a halt.

Plantations of young trees criss-crossed the foreground, their grey-green leaves stirred by the light breeze. With a sudden stab of guilt, she recognised how her ignorance of straying cattle had endangered the project.

No wonder Josh Logan had been angry, was still angry. The whole district knew about her thoughtlessness in spoiling the film shoot, but they had laughed it off. Josh couldn't. Her city ways had put all this at risk and he probably wondered what she might do next.

It was quite a while before Meredith realised the engine was still running. She glanced at the distant house. There was no need to go any farther, no need to ask his wife for an explanation. Moving the gear stick into drive, she turned the car on the narrow road.

The decision to seek answers to her questions had been a good one. Meredith found her action had somehow freed up her thinking and when she returned to the computer the words began to flow from her fingers.

The shadows were long in the garden before she gave up with an exasperated sigh. She had made some progress but it gave her very little satisfaction. She'd dealt with enough manuscripts to know the writing was stilted, the characters lifeless. What was wrong with her?

She realised that at this rate she would take more than three months to write her novel. That meant more time off work, and more money would be needed. Where would that come from? She was tightly budgeted as it was. The prospects were gloomy.

A car was coming down the road from the entrance gate. She expected it would be Josh Logan returning to his family in the hidden valley. She shook off the faint twinge of envy. Why should the thought affect her?

Family life was not for her. She'd made that choice long ago when she'd fled a dysfunctional foster family and made a new start in a new city, among strangers.

She'd worked hard in her chosen job and succeeded, and believed there wasn't anything she couldn't do, if she tried. That included writing a novel.

The car stopped, there was the sound of the garden gate latch clicking and steps on the veranda. Her heartbeat edged up a notch. What could Josh want? Was there a chance he'd know she'd been on the road to his house?

She'd heard him go by early in the morning, presumably on the way to school, or filming. Had his wife seen her car and reported it? And how would he take that? As an invasion of his privacy? It certainly wouldn't endear her to him.

The front door opened and a cheery voice called, 'Hello, anyone home?'

All the tension left Meredith's body. Why should she have imagined it would be her neighbour? He wouldn't be coming by. She went down the hallway to welcome Rob Hurst.

He stood large in the doorway, a baker's basket hooked over one forearm, and a table napkin over the other. 'Room service, ma'am.'

'How did you know I'd forgotten all about dinner?' she asked, waving him towards the kitchen.

'I figured a writer might do that.'

Meredith sighed. 'I wish I could claim the title of writer.'

His eyes twinkled above the bushy beard. 'Don't tell me being a novelist is hard.'

'Stop teasing me,' she retorted. 'It certainly isn't easy.'

'So? Haven't you heard the saying that life wasn't meant to be easy?' He was unpacking the basket as he spoke.

Meredith exclaimed with pleasure as he laid the contents on the table. She lifted the lid on the casserole. 'Ah, coq au vin! My favourite.'

Rob turned on the oven and placed the still-warm casserole in it. He found two glasses, uncorked the wine and poured it before turning to her for approval.

She clapped her hands. 'Good boy,' she cried getting into the spirit of the moment. It was such a change from her mood prior to his arrival.

'But wait, there's more!'

He removed the cling-wrap from the plate of canapés and offered them.

'Shall we be more sophisticated and adjourn to the sitting room?' She led the way out of the kitchen.

After a quick check of the oven reading, Rob followed her.

It wasn't until the meal was over and they were nibbling cheese that the talk turned to his work day.

'Beards are a nuisance,' he confided, carefully dabbing at the corners of his mouth with his napkin. 'They need a lot of attention. Time consuming.'

Meredith smiled at the picture of Rob dragging a comb through the bushiness every morning.

'I imagine it would be easy for a bird to mistake it for a nesting place. Have you looked under it lately?'

The talk of beards seemed the starting place for Rob. As their shared laughter died, he poured the last of the wine into her glass and leaned forward.

'Have you changed your mind about appearing in the film?'

Disappointment shafted through Meredith. This hadn't been a generous visit, a thoughtful gesture. It was planned with a specific goal in mind.

'I seem to have forgotten a basic rule,' she said, rising from the table and gathering up the used plates with unnecessary vigour. 'Beware of Greeks who come bearing gifts,' she quoted over her shoulder as she disappeared into the kitchen.

'Meredith!' he called as he followed her. 'What is it with you?'

Some of her annoyance had already drained away, replaced by a weariness. What did it matter? She'd never fit in. The best thing to do was to stick to her plan, write the novel and return to the city.

She swung round from the sink and faced him. 'It's you country people,' she explained. 'We couldn't enjoy a quiet dinner in a civilised way, oh, no, there had to be a reason for it. In this case, to get me to fall in with your film-making plans. I can't imagine why you are so keen for that to happen. There must be hundreds of star-struck women dying for the chance.'

He took a step toward her. 'You don't get it, do you?'

6

For a moment Meredith wondered if she should be afraid. After all, she didn't know Rob Hurst very well and they were alone in an isolated cottage, with help a mile away in the township. And her car locked in the garage.

Josh Logan's house was closer. Perhaps she could run there, but he'd shown so little interest in her welfare it probably would be useless appealing to him. Given she made it in the dark. Her breath caught in her throat.

Rob stopped in the middle of the room and stared at her, his brows drawn together in a frown.

'You really don't get it,' he repeated, shaking his head as if in wonderment. She could see she'd been wrong about him — he was no threat to her, only a puzzle.

Thankfully she wouldn't have to seek

help after all, she began to breathe more easily. 'Whatever do you mean? What don't I get?' she asked.

'You had a good time at the dinner?'

'Once it got going,' she admitted ruefully.

'Other people enjoyed it, too.'

'I'm so glad for you,' she said and immediately regretted the sarcastic tone. After all, he had brought dinner. 'As the host, you must have been pleased,' she added, trying to make amends.

'I'm saying they enjoyed your performance. You'd be surprised how many thought you were fun. Everyone, in fact. They wanted to get to know you better, and were expecting to. On the film set.'

Rob was making sense at last. 'This is the country, remember,' he went on. 'The whole township is involved with the filming — you're the only one not there. That bothers them. They don't want you to feel out of it.'

'Are you suggesting I'm letting the side down?'

'Something like that.'

Meredith let herself relax back against the bench and began laughing. How foolish she'd been to feel threatened. He probably didn't even fancy her, despite Chloe's wildly romantic ideas. 'I'm flattered, but there's my writing . . .'

'Couldn't you handle both? I imagine you're capable of doing more than one thing at a time. Generally speaking, women are good at it, and I suspect that goes for you more than most.'

'You're doing well, you know. Flattery will get you everything.'

He laughed confidently. 'Yes, I know'

* * *

The sound of female voices carried on the early morning air as Meredith and her escort approached the little church hall.

Inside, a crowd of women in various stages of undress queued to be assessed and handed suitable outfits from the racks of costumes lining the walls.

The arrival of a man in their midst raised the level of excitement another notch. The director's assistant took no notice of their squeals and led her through the crush to the clothes-filled kitchen.

'Martin's wife,' he said to the woman seated at a table. As she rose and came to meet Meredith, he gave a nod of farewell and was gone.

'I'm Jacinta, the wardrobe mistress. Although I saw you at Rob's party, you won't mind if I call you by your character's name on the set, will you? It's common practice. And easier for me.'

'I'd better know who I am, then. Who is Martin?'

Jacinta consulted her information sheet.

'Martin is one of Mad Dog's brothers, Mad Dog being the bushranger. The whole family are engaged in robbery-under-arms, as the crime was known in those days. Your name is Rose.'

She tugged the tape measure from

around her neck and efficiently com-
piled a list of Meredith's vital statistics
before making choices from the rack.
She reeled them off, one by one, as
she piled Meredith's arms high with
clothes.

'Long calico petticoat, long skirt,
high-necked blouse, shawl and — ' She
perched a gingham bonnet on Meredith's
head. 'One bonnet.'

Meredith moved away to make room
for the next person.

'Your feet!' the wardrobe mistress
exclaimed from behind her. 'Don't you
have boots? We're not supplying them.
Didn't think we'd need to, out here in
the country. Get dressed first and then
go find Rob — he'll sell you a pair.'

Meredith laughed. 'He's been trying
to do that since I arrived.'

★   ★   ★

By the time she was dressed and had
been through the make-up marquee,
the cast and crew were having a break

98

for morning coffee. They milled around the mobile kitchen parked behind the church. She knew where Rob Hurst would be and crossed the road to the hardware store, walking awkwardly as she adjusted to the voluminous skirt.

'My, don't you look fetching,' he greeted her, clearing the chair opposite him of newspapers, and pouring an extra cup of coffee.

'The first time I sat in this chair I didn't dream I was going to be involved in film making,' Meredith mused.

'You're not sorry already, are you?' he asked.

'Well, no, I'm not. As you said, everyone has been very . . . very welcoming.' She could have added, except Josh Logan, but didn't.

'It's the — '

'Country way,' she joined in.

★ ★ ★

The store had a good range of boots in all sizes. And Rob had the good manners, or the wisdom, not to remind her he'd told her she'd need them.

Standing in front of the mirror and getting the first full view of herself, she agreed with him — she did look fetching. In an old-fashioned way.

'I'm Rose, Martin's wife. I wonder who will be playing the part of Martin?' she asked Rob's reflection.

Without answering, he busied himself packing boots back into matching boxes and replacing them on the shelves behind her.

She turned away from the mirror.

'Rob, you must know who it is. Tell me! Is he one of the locals?'

He nodded, continuing with his task.

'Yes, as a matter of fact. It isn't a big part. Martin has to be seen a lot in family scenes but not heard often. They found someone suitable locally, didn't have to bring in an actor.'

'Then why don't you tell me what he's like.'

He couldn't make his job last any longer. The final box in its proper place, he had to face her.

'He's a very quiet sort of fellow, keeps to himself . . . '

'Good looking?'

'Yes, good looking, even with a beard.' A hooter sounded. He glanced at his watch. 'The break is over, we'd better get back.'

★ ★ ★

There was a Hollywood-ish air on the usually quiet street. Stefan sat in a director's chair at the centre of the activity, a French beret covering his shaven head. A bevy of assistants hovered around him, taking their orders and executing them promptly.

Assistants were organising the extras at both ends of the street, another was instructing them by means of a loud hailer.

'Now, what this is about is the bushranger family has come to town and the townsfolk are alarmed. When I call action, I want you to scurry about doing whatever you're supposed to be doing.'

'Don't worry too much just now, we'll have a practice run first,' he assured them. 'And in the meantime, will members of the Morgan family please assemble at Ritchie's garage.'

Meredith turned her head to say farewell to Rob, but he had disappeared. A sizeable knot of people had gathered outside the garage and was growing. There was nothing to indicate the Hollywood star was already there.

She imagined him being fussed over inside the building or even in a location caravan somewhere, waiting to emerge when everything had been set up for the shoot and the cameras were ready to roll.

She joined the group. Apart from the lighting and camera crews, it seemed to comprise mostly of women and children and only one or two bearded men.

From the outer edges of the gathering, Meredith stretched herself on tip-toes to get a better view of the man in charge. She felt a pair of strong hands seize her waist from behind and hoist her off her feet, holding her close to his shoulder.

'There, now you can see,' said a voice muffled by her voluminous skirt.

Flustered by this display of country friendliness, she put out a hand to control some of its fullness and bent her head to look down into the face of her benefactor.

Twinkling eyes above a silky, brown beard met hers. A faint hope stirred her senses. Perhaps he'd turn out to be her screen husband, Martin. It would make for an interesting day if she were so lucky.

The assistant director began his briefing. 'The Morgan family have come into town, women and children in the wagon. The men will be on horseback, Mad Dog, the undisputed leader of the clan, out in front. Where are you, Mad Dog?' he called, his eyes raking the group.

'I'll have to put you down,' murmured the man as he lowered Meredith to the ground and shouldered his way to the centre of the group.

The assistant director acknowledged the presence of his Hollywood big-name actor. 'Good. Now, one of the women will be driving the wagon. I've no doubt you country people can all handle horses . . . '

'I think the one in the pink blouse and the gingham bonnet should do the driving,' Mad Dog suggested. 'She'd look good on camera as they come into focus at the top of the street.'

The assistant director looked as if he might agree to his star's suggestion. Already feeling silly at not recognising such a well-known movieland identity, Meredith was dismayed as the attention of the whole group swung on to her.

'No, no, I can't drive a horse and cart!' she cried, the very thought knotting her stomach nerves.

'There's nothing to it,' Mad Dog insisted, taking her hand. 'You drive a car, think of this as just an old-fashioned people-mover.' The men laughed at his witticism.

★　★　★

The wagon, a simple, dray-like cart with basic wooden seating, was standing on the street. An old-fashioned people-mover? Mad Dog was right about that, but as to easy driving . . .

As they walked towards it a horse was being brought forward and backed between the shafts.

Meredith regarded the animal with horror. It was big. And it was smelly, even from a distance.

The women in the group began to show their concern for her.

'She can't do it, she's a townie!' they chorused.

An old woman with a weather-beaten face pushed to the front and took charge. 'I'm playing Ma Morgan,' she said to Meredith. 'You sit beside me, that way everyone will be satisfied. The cameraman will have a pretty face filling his lens, the horses won't bolt and we'll stay sweet with Mad Dog.' She winked and lowered her voice. 'And you won't be made to look like a fool.'

A wave of relief washed over Meredith and calmed her fears. Grateful to the old woman, she clutched at her skirt with one hand, grabbed the handrail with the other and climbed up into the wagon.

Ma Morgan followed, settling herself in the driver's seat.

'Ready!' She called to the assistant director.

From her perch, Meredith could see the bewildered look on his face that said it all. He didn't know how, but the whole matter had been taken out of his hands. Most satisfactorily.

Women power, she thought. Country women power! She felt like cheering.

'Er, yes. Good.' He seemed to make a big effort to regain control. 'All the women and little ones get into the cart, please, and you big kids can run behind it if there's not enough room.'

Men on horseback had appeared at the rear of one of the buildings and were being marshalled to take their place. The make-up girls clambered among the women with last-minute dabs at shiny noses.

Meredith thought of Chloe. She hadn't seen her all morning. Had the hairdresser been able to wake up in time to help with the extras?

Perhaps there was another marquee somewhere behind the main street.

Suddenly, there was order out of the confusion. All eyes were on the Hollywood actor playing Mad Dog Morgan.

He certainly looked the part, sitting straight and arrogant in the saddle. Not at all like the real person she'd met. A handler led his horse to the head of the group, the other riders falling into line behind him, on either side of the cart.

A horse snorted in Meredith's ear.

She drew back against Ma Morgan's ample body in fright and lifted startled eyes to its rider.

Josh Logan raised the battered felt hat he wore. 'Martin Morgan, ma'am.'

7

Meredith's first thoughts were of Rob Hurst. The wretched man had known all along the role that she would be taking in the film. And with whom she'd be paired! And he had known she wouldn't have agreed to do it under those circumstances, despite all his flattery and talk of country friendliness. No way!

Despite the dilemma of being partnered with a man who'd shown little interest in her, Meredith felt the pull of the story being recreated more than a hundred years after it happened.

The loudspeaker boomed down the street. 'Places, everybody. We're going to do a run-through. Don't move until I call 'Action'!'

The street was silent except for the low murmurings between the crew on their walkie-talkies. Meredith put aside thoughts of Josh Logan and willed herself to be Rose Morgan, with her husband, Martin, riding beside her. It was the only way she'd get through the day. Until she met up with Rob Hurst!

'Clear the set! . . . Action!'

Suddenly, there was movement. Ma Morgan shouted, 'Giddup!' and slapped the reins sharply against the horse's rump. The wagon creaked forward, following Mad Dog into town.

It wasn't the smoothest ride Meredith had experienced nor the most comfortable of seats, but that seemed to add authenticity to the scene. She held on to the iron side-rail as they rumbled past the shops and suitably apprehensive townsfolk.

'Cut!' came the order as the Morgan family group reached the bottom of the street, and broke up.

'OK,' called the disembodied voice. 'That was only a practice run. Now we'll go through it again but this time the men will dismount and tie their horses to the hitching rail. Everybody back to their places, please.'

There were smiles all round as the handlers led the horses back to the starting point, and the inexperienced extras took up their original positions. Meredith wondered how long the smiles would last if Stefan demanded too many retakes. It could become very boring.

Back at the starting point, the assistant director came around the wagon to stand between it and Josh's mount, and began stroking the animal's nose.

'Stefan thinks the shot lacks oomph,' he said, a quick glance encompassing both Josh and Meredith before concentrating on the horse again.

She felt the first stirrings of misgivings. Lacks oomph? The film wasn't about oomph, it was about Australian history.

'And how do you intend to give it oomph,' she asked.

'Stefan has suggested Rose ride up front of Martin on his horse.' Meredith's darkening face must have warned him the idea was not being well-received. He began to make excuses. 'That'll leave more room in the wagon . . . '

She looked to Josh for his support but, as usual, his bearded face told her nothing. Obviously, he wouldn't like it any more than she did but clearly, if anything was to be done, it was up to her.

'Ride up front on his horse?' she repeated, trying to sound calm and reasonable despite the fluttering of butterflies in her stomach. 'Doesn't that defeat the purpose of frightening the townsfolk? They'd hardly be scared of someone . . . ' She searched for the right words. 'Someone with his arms around his . . . woman.'

Josh spoke at last. 'I think Rose has a point,' he said, avoiding Meredith's eyes and looking straight at the assistant director. 'A bushranger wouldn't be likely to show such . . . er . . . such softness. Not in public.'

The man was uncomfortable. 'It's

what Stefan wants,' he said.

The idea of riding up front on a horse in Josh Logan's arms was more than Meredith could contemplate.

She climbed from the wagon and strode down the street. Pushing past the technical staff gathered around the director, she stood in front of his eyeline and confronted him.

If she'd imagined she was someone special to Stefan because he'd singled her out at the party, she was mistaken. He showed no sign of recognition.

'Yes?' he barked impatiently.

'I don't think much of your idea of oomph — '

'Oomph?' Stefan looked for enlightenment from his crew. They acted as if they'd never heard the word before. 'Who is this woman?' he demanded.

'One of the Morgan wives — '

Meredith cut across the assistant's reply. 'This business of wanting me to ride up front of . . . my husband on his horse — '

Stefan was still looking bewildered.

'What is she on about?' he asked of no-one in particular, a querulous note creeping into his voice.

The nervous assistant offered an explanation.

'I think she's talking about your idea of romancing up that scene, Stefan.'

Meredith could see the director wasn't used to his work being questioned and certainly not by some bit player. His face was thunderous.

She looked away. 'Where's Rob,' she asked, her eyes scanning the crew.

Another assistant stepped forward, and, with his hand on her elbow, urged her away. 'Rob's gone to the city to pick up the leading lady from the airport.'

She hated to give up, but without him acting as a go-between there was nothing she could do. Somehow she must get through the scene — and the day. Josh Logan would have to put up with it, too.

'Rob's gone to the city,' she informed him when she got back to the wagon.

A handler was waiting beside the

horse, his knees slightly bent, his hands locked together in front of himself.

Meredith stared at him for a long while before she realised that was where she was expected to put her foot. 'Are you going to heave me up on to the horse? In this skirt? Impossible.'

The horse moved restlessly, alarming her.

Josh quietened it with a pat on the neck, and leaned down from the saddle. 'Not if you ride side-saddle. Now, turn your back to me,' he instructed. 'Put one foot in Rodney's hands and steady yourself on his shoulders. He'll hoist you up.'

The wooden plank that was the wagon's seat had been hard and unforgiving, but to Meredith's surprise, the horse's back was well-padded, its shiny coat smooth to the touch.

Josh's arms circled her loosely to hold the slack reins.

Thankfully, I don't have to look him in the face, she thought, spreading her skirt. That would be too much.

The assistant director came to check the new arrangement, and the readiness of the Morgan family, before speaking into his walkie-talkie.

'Action!' boomed the loud speakers.

The horse's pleasant gait as they got under way was another surprise for Meredith. She allowed herself to become Rose Morgan and relaxed against her screen husband.

There was a sudden distraction to one side of the street, as two dogs on the pavement began fighting. Locked in a snarling, biting embrace, they tumbled across the road in front of the Morgan cavalcade.

The leading horse whinnied and reared up on its hind legs in fright, the actor playing Mad Dog pulling hard on shortened reins to control it and stay on its back.

Behind him, the other horses shied and broke away in all directions, colliding with each other in the melee.

Meredith's make-believe world of Rose and Martin was shattered. Under them, their mount heaved and backed away. A tiny scream escaped her lips as, fearful of being thrown, both her hands went out in a frantic grab for the spooked animal's mane. She felt one of Josh's arms tighten around her, pulling her back hard against his body, holding her there.

At the same time, he deftly combined the two reins in his right hand, taking up the slack and managing to edge the horse through the chaos of startled animals on to the pavement.

★ ★ ★

When order was restored, an announcement was made over the loud speakers. 'We'll break for lunch early, folks.' A relieved murmur rippled through the crowd.

'You're trembling!' Josh exclaimed.

Meredith half-turned in his arms, to face the concerned look in his eyes. 'It was frightening,' she admitted.

And it had been, but it was over. Why

wasn't her heartbeat slowing?

'Let's go to lunch,' he suggested.

'I'm not getting down from here just to be hauled up again,' she declared emphatically.

'Could I bring you something to eat, then?' he asked.

Meredith stared at him. Was he sending her up? What little she could see of his face was serious enough, but soon little lines crinkled around his eyes. They deepened and, as if he couldn't help himself, he was laughing. She realised how ridiculous she was being and joined in.

He dismounted and held up his arms to her. Still laughing, she slid down into them.

★ ★ ★

Meredith was already at her personal computer the next morning looking for inspiration when Chloe rang. 'Are you coming to town this morning?' the hairdresser asked.

'No, I haven't been called for today. In fact, I'm not sure I have any more appearances scheduled. Yesterday may have been my one big chance for stardom.'

'And what a meal you made of it, up close and personal with the school teacher, no less,' Chloe teased.

Meredith was glad Chloe couldn't see the flush that rose up her neck. At times it had been very personal, especially when the horses shied.

She didn't know what to make of the changed relationship between herself and Josh.

'Oh, Chloe, you and your romantic ideas! We were literally thrown together — '

'And almost thrown off together, I hear,' interrupted the hairdresser. 'It was lucky no-one was injured. But what I rang about is this — Angelique, the film star, flew in from America yesterday and the national press are coming to interview and photograph her on the set today. We're all going for a look-see. Why don't you come?'

Meredith was ready with her standard refusal of having to get on with her writing but Chloe was determined.

'Come on, it'll be fun,' she urged. 'All the kids are mad keen to get her autograph.'

A Hollywood starlet was of little interest to Meredith, but connections had been made with the locals during her day on the set. When the assistant director finally declared a wrap as the light faded, the spirit of camaraderie persisted in the changing room.

She had come home with a sheaf of invitations from her new friends. 'I guess my novel will still be here tomorrow,' she admitted, not without a twinge of guilt at her lack of discipline. 'Where did this Angelique stay last night?'

'At Rob's,' Chloe replied. 'There aren't any hotels around here, so all the crew are billeted with locals. Now, are you coming?'

Meredith gave in. 'Oh, all right. I'll be there right away.'

★ ★ ★

The street was busy with cars and vans, some emblazoned with the logos of city television stations. Meredith parked behind Chloe's salon and knocked on the back door. The sound of excited children's voices reached her as it opened.

'How many children do you have, Chloe?' she asked.

'They're not all mine, thank goodness. I don't have a spare room for a billet as such, but, with the school closed during filming, I've taken a couple of kids in with mine to leave their folk free. The film company is paying the Mothers' Club. That's my contribution.'

She clapped her hands for order. 'Come on, kids, Meredith is here. Let's all go see Angelique.'

There were only five children, all girls, but it seemed like more to Meredith. They quickly replaced the combs and brushes they'd been playing with and gathered their belongings. A little figure with a familiar junior back-pack detached herself and came to stand beside her.

'Hello, Meredith.'

'Cassie! What are you doing here?'

'I'm having a holiday with Chloe's family.'

The child's eyes lit up. 'I get to sleep in a bunk! The top one.'

'She's enjoying the company,' Chloe murmured in an aside, as she shepherded the chattering girls through the door of the salon, pulling it closed behind them.

Meredith was puzzled. There was something odd about the arrangement. Why wasn't the child with her uncle's family, in his house?

She wished she'd known about this yesterday, she could have asked Josh. He certainly was more approachable than on previous occasions. In fact, after the initial wariness they had established a rapport she hadn't thought possible.

She smiled. It was all to do with

having a similar sense of humour, she told herself. An important ingredient in any relationship, neighbourly or otherwise. And nothing to do with sooty eyelashes.

A little hand slipped into hers as they walked along the pavement. Meredith looked down at the eager face.

'I'm so glad to see you again,' Cassie confided. 'When I come home I'll tell you all about Chloe's house.'

'I heard that,' Chloe teased. 'Sounds as if you're in for a session of 'Show and Tell', Meredith.'

It seemed as if the whole district had gathered in the township, the street crowded with people all going in the same direction. Meredith greeted several of her new friends.

The press conference was being held out in the open. A table had been set up on the median strip at the top of the street, ensuring a photographic backdrop of the old-fashioned township.

Stefan sat at the table, flanked by his Hollywood stars, the bearded Mad Dog

Morgan and his love interest, the sultry Angelique. The film company's press officer, also an American, opened the proceedings by introducing the stars. The photographers crouched at their feet, clicking furiously.

Meredith was surprised Rob wasn't in charge. He stood to one side, his eyes on Angelique. And why not? The girl was lovely. It would interesting to see how Stefan twisted the film's story to include a love interest.

The little hand in hers tugged for attention. Meredith bent down to hear the whispered request. 'Meredith, I need to go to the toilet.'

The walk back to the hairdressing salon didn't take long. In typical Warrawilla fashion, the door was unlocked. There was no need to wonder should she offer her assistance to the self-possessed little girl. Cassie disappeared into the back rooms.

On their return, Meredith led the way around the crowd towards where Rob was standing. Although the day filming with Josh had turned out quite well, she still wanted to tell Rob she hadn't appreciated the trick he'd played on her. It could easily have been disastrous.

'Why, hello, ladies. Come to see the film stars, eh?' He bent and lifted Cassie up for a quick look before letting her down. 'Sorry I can't hold you there for long, Cassie. You're growing so fast.'

'Did you know Chloe has a pony on her farm?' Cassie asked. 'And an emu.'

Rob gave Meredith a quick grin. 'Obviously film stars don't rate very highly with Cassie. I should have saved my strength,' he murmured before answering the little girl.

The press officer announced the second stage of the photo opportunity would feature the horsemen and was to take place in the stockyards just off the main street. The photographers packed their gear and moved away. The crowd followed.

'Uncle Josh is a good horse rider. He's going to teach me when I'm bigger,' Cassie informed them, skipping ahead.

Talk of horse-riding reminded Meredith of her day on the movie set and of Rob's part in organising it. 'I wasn't too thrilled with the secretive way you paired me up with Josh,' she complained. 'It was embarrassing. For both of us.'

'Josh was embarrassed? I find that hard to believe. It was his suggestion.'

8

A surge of good-natured townsfolk was carrying them forward, when all Meredith wanted to do was stand still for a moment and have Rob's undivided attention. What was he saying?

She put out a hand and grabbed his sleeve. 'Wait! What do you mean it was his suggestion? Why would he do that?'

He stopped and let the others go past. 'Why are you so surprised? Didn't you get along well?'

'Well, yes, we did. He's . . . a very nice person, not at all as I expected.'

Rob raised his eyebrows at that.

'He hadn't shown a liking for my company before. In fact, just the opposite,' she explained.

He shook his head. 'I can't believe you two. So he's shy. I told you he was a bit of a loner, that he kept pretty well to himself.'

Meredith couldn't remember having been told that, and shy wasn't a word she'd apply to Josh. There was a certain confidence about him that didn't fit that description. To her, it seemed more like a wariness. But why? Perhaps something in his past had caused that.

Shyness or wariness, what did it matter? She felt farther away than ever from understanding country people and country men in particular.

As they neared the stockyards she made a decision, she wasn't going to try any more. 'Will you see Cassie gets back to Chloe, please, Rob?' she asked, calling the little girl for a hug, and transferring her hand to his. 'I have something to do.'

Something more important, she told herself. What being in Warrawilla was all about — she had a novel to write.

The days were passing and she'd not made much progress. She got into the car and drove back towards Mile End.

She thought of Josh as the gate swung easily on its hinges. It reminded her of the day of its installation. He had been so off-hand as to be almost rude. She'd imagined it was lingering anger because of the cattle. After their day together on the film set she was certain it hadn't been shyness. Something else must be behind it.

And now Rob was claiming Josh had asked to be partnered with her for the filming. It just didn't make sense.

Neither did her writing. At the end of the afternoon Meredith was not satisfied with her work. Reading it over, she had to wonder was coming to the country to write a novel a pie-in-the-sky idea? Instead of peace and quiet, she'd become involved with the townsfolk and the making of a film. It hadn't been good for concentration, and that showed.

Doubts entered her mind. Was her dream of becoming a writer just that — a dream? Was there more to being a novelist than just sitting at the computer? Could this be something she couldn't conquer by will-power and hard work, as she'd done with every-thing else in her life?

Still questioning herself, she stepped through the French windows into the garden and walked to its farthermost boundary. Beyond the fence the heavily-wooded land sloped upwards in the beginnings of the foothills.

For the first time since arriving, she felt the urge to explore. She wondered how high she'd have to climb before there was any kind of a view.

The shadows were lengthening and the trees in the garden were full of twittering, rustling birds. Above the din, she picked up the sound of an engine idling, only one, so different from the roar of the evening peak-hour city traffic in her other life.

From where she stood she could see it was Josh at the entrance to the property. Meredith watched as the tall figure got out of the truck to open the gate, and back in to drive through, then repeat the action to close it. Her spirits lifted at the sight of him. It was good that they were friends.

She hoped he might stop for a chat, but why should he? He was going home to his family. Meredith wondered what his wife was like and why she wasn't taking part in the filming. Were there small children keeping her housebound? There were all sorts of questions.

In a single, clarifying moment, her confidence returned. This was why she couldn't write — her head was a mish-mash of unanswerable questions. It was no good telling herself an interest in people was supposed to be the sign of a good writer. The truth was she'd been procrastinating.

Determined to apply herself more rigorously to her writing, Meredith was up early the next morning, but not earlier than some.

She was on her first cup of coffee when Chloe rang. 'You're on the front page!'

'Whatever are you talking about, Chloe? Getting up early doesn't suit you. Slow down.'

'The city newspapers have arrived and there's a beautiful photo of the three of you — '

'The three of who?'

'Rob is holding Cassie up high to see Angelique, and you're there beside him. You'd better come in right away before all the papers are sold. There are more photos of the township in the back pages so I expect they'll sell out quickly.'

Meredith felt the temptation to abandon her work, but resisted. She had turned over a new leaf. 'Why don't you buy one to keep for me,' she suggested. 'I'll come for it tomorrow.'

★ ★ ★

The shrill ringing tones sounded like an alarm to Meredith. Groggy with sleep, she stretched out an arm in the darkness to silence it, not yet ready to obey its imperative. Her tentative fingers discovered her bedside reading, a glass of water, and eventually, a button on the digital clock/radio. She pressed it down, but the noise didn't stop.

It took some time for her to waken sufficiently to read the display panel. Midnight! Her mind registered that the incessant sound was coming from the telephone in the kitchen. There was a brief break as the call fell out, before it began ringing again. Someone was determined to reach her, but who could it be at this time of the night?

She slipped her feet into her scuffs and shuffled through to answer. 'Meredith, it's Josh Logan here. Sorry to be phoning at this time, but may I come and see you? Please, it's urgent.'

Not completely free of sleep, Meredith struggled to understand.

'Come and see me?' she repeated. 'It's urgent?'

'Yes, very urgent.'

'Can't you tell me over the phone?'

'Meredith!'

The urgency in his voice decided for her. 'Of course, you can come.'

Meredith dressed and was waiting on the veranda when the dark bulk of the truck, with no lights showing, emerged out of the night from the direction of the gate.

She was surprised. A midnight telephone call, driving without lights? What was happening? She was even more surprised when Josh opened the passenger side door and carried the sleeping form of Cassie into the house.

'Put her in my bed,' Meredith urged, fussing anxiously behind him, expecting him to undress the child and tuck her in.

Instead, he laid her on the rumpled bed without taking her shoes off, and covered her gently with the duvet. 'Her clothes . . . ?'

'Later, Meredith, later,' he answered, switching off the light and leading the way out of the room.

To Meredith, the night was taking on an unreal aspect. Automatically, she went through the motions of making coffee. Josh watched her, and waited until she finished before he spoke.

'It's about the photo.' He dived a hand into an inside coat pocket, and brought out a page of a newspaper. He laid it on the table and smoothed out the creases.

The photo was a beautiful study of Cassie's animated face as Rob held her high on his shoulder to get a glimpse of the Hollywood starlet. Not that Angelique had been the reason for the child's animation, as Meredith remembered with a smile. The animals on Chloe's farm had been the cause of the excitement.

'What does this photo have to do with . . . ' Her voice trailed off as she looked at Josh.

'It's brought about a situation, a threatening situation.'

'Threatening to whom?'

'To Cassie.' He got up from the table and began pacing the room. 'We are not quite as we seem. Cassie is my sister's child. Divorce proceedings had begun when the father, Don, was killed in a car accident. That would have been complicated enough, but his parents are taking my sister to the Family Court, asking for custody. They claim Don would have won if the divorce had gone ahead.

'That's hardly likely — the courts usually favour the mother unless she's proved neglectful. My sister was a busy, but loving mother.'

He paused, looked into his coffee mug and found it empty. 'Any chance of another?' he asked.

'Of course.' Meredith was glad of the break in his recital to take in the little he had already told her. He still hadn't explained the connection with the photo but it was a start.

Josh took a gulp from the re-filled mug and went on.

'The in-laws weren't happy with the way things were going in court and made threats about taking the law into their own hands. My sister became frightened for Cassie, who was just then starting school. There had been a similar case widely reported in the media where a child had been kidnapped by grandparents, hidden, and given a new identity.'

Meredith was dismayed by the story. That Cassie should be harassed and for her mother to fear for the child's safety was unthinkable. 'But couldn't the police protect her?' she asked.

'They can't do anything unless a criminal act has been committed. The in-laws were clever. It was silent intimidation.'

'But that doesn't seem fair,' she protested.

'That's how it is. I figured there was only one thing to do. I changed my name, got a job as a teacher here and brought Cassie with me. Just until it's all over and she can get back with her mother.

'I've had to be careful with strangers, and hope this place is so far removed from her home that they wouldn't know where to start looking. That's how it's been. Until this photo appeared on the front page of a city newspaper.'

He slumped in the chair, the strain of his concern for Cassie showing.

Meredith didn't know what to say that would be of any comfort to him. She was busy putting two and two together and coming up with some answers but not enough of them to satisfy her completely. His fear of strangers explained his reticence toward her when they first met, but what was he doing here now?

'Josh, what does you being here with Cassie mean?'

He got up and came to stand beside her. 'It means I trust your feelings for the child,' he replied.

'You're right about that. I've taken a liking to her. But what can I do to help?'

'Would you look after her?'

Although surprised by this midnight request, Meredith didn't hesitate. 'Of course she can stay with me. I'll love having her. Perhaps she will help me with my storytelling.'

There was no change to the serious-ness of Josh's face. 'I need you to take her back to the city with you,' he said. 'And look after her there.'

The idea appealed to Meredith. It was a long drive and she would be glad of the child's company when the time came. And afterwards, if needed. 'I'll take her. No trouble. She'll be very welcome when I go.'

'Tonight.'

'Tonight?'

'Yes.'

Her breath caught in her throat at the unexpectedness of that. 'It's a big ask, Josh,' she protested, looking into his desperate eyes. 'Why tonight?'

'They're here already. Rob warned me there were questions being asked in the store this afternoon. The trouble is he and I are both contracted to filming for a couple more days and can't leave. Then I thought of you. We agreed you would be just the person to ask. After dinner, I went out to Chloe's and brought Cassie away with me.'

He ran his fingers through his thick hair. 'Luckily, Chloe and the townsfolk know nothing, but it will only be a matter of time before the strangers learn there's a schoolteacher living on his own with a little girl — '

'Living on his own? Aren't you married with a family?'

9

Clearly, her question interrupted the flow of Josh's thoughts. A frown creased his forehead.

'Sorry, what was that?' he asked.

It seemed to Meredith that he was taking a long time to answer but given his pre-occupation with Cassie, she had to admit that was unfair of her.

Before she could remind herself of the reason for her being in Warrawilla, and of its short-lived nature, a wide-awake Cassie came through the door. 'Is Meredith going to look after me, Uncle Josh?' she asked, going to him.

Josh nodded.

'Oh goody! But I'll need to change into my pyjamas, won't I? And take off my shoes. You shouldn't have put me to bed with my shoes on, Uncle Josh.'

Josh crouched down and drew the little girl into the circle of his arms. 'I did that because I wasn't sure if Meredith would . . . er . . . I had to ask her first.'

'That's good manners, isn't it?'

'Yes, Possum, it's good manners.' He glanced up at Meredith with the trace of a smile in his eyes. 'Meredith is going to drive you back to the city tonight so there's no need to change.'

Meredith felt she'd missed something, she hadn't agreed to that. She was a competent driver but the thought of negotiating her way in darkness along the unfamiliar back roads until they joined the highway, was daunting.

'I'm sorry, Josh, I can't do that till the morning,' she said. What he asked of her had sent her mind into fast-forward, past the actual drive to the city — to her life there. Surely this was a sign. Was it time to be honest with herself and admit she'd never be a writer, that it had been an impossible dream?

'It'll take me that long to pack up, anyway,' she added.

He looked as if it was the last thing

he'd expected. Disbelief replaced amusement in his eyes. 'What do you mean, pack up?'

'It's just that when I go back to the city, it will be for good. I've been thinking about it and have realised I made a mistake in coming here. I'm definitely not a country person, very much a fish out of water.' She smiled ruefully at him, wishing it wasn't true. 'And I'm not a writer, I can see that.'

Josh and Cassie both looked as if they would protest but Meredith had made her decision. She did what she did best — she began to organise.

'I suggest we get some sleep. You'll need it, Josh, if you're to be filming in the morning, and I have to be fresh for the long drive.'

'It isn't true, you're not like a fish out of water, Meredith. If you were you'd be gasping,' Cassie insisted. 'Like this.' She made fish-faces.

Laughing, Meredith took the child's hand. 'Come along, I'll undress you while Uncle Josh brings in your suitcase.'

* * *

Morning came sooner than Meredith wished. Beside her in the bed, the little girl slept on. The care of the child was a big responsibility, especially as she'd gone against Josh's original proposal by delaying her departure until the daylight hours. She hoped she'd done the right thing.

The night before, with Cassie tucked in, and already dropping off to sleep, the work of packing up had begun, ready for an early start.

'They won't come tonight, even if they know where to look for you, which I doubt,' Meredith had reasoned. 'The shops in Warrawilla won't be open much before eight, so who will give them the information they need?'

'The film crew are on the streets just after daybreak — '

'How many of them know Cassie is connected to you?' she asked.

Josh had to admit very few, if any. 'She stayed with Chloe's family on the farm during the filming, quite happy and safe there.' He sighed. 'Until the older girls wanted to see that starlet, Angelique. Chloe wasn't to know this would happen.'

The good sense of her argument seemed to quieten his anxieties. He followed her lead in clearing the rooms of her belongings. Soon boxes and bags were piled near the front door ready for packing the car once daylight came.

At last, everything that could be done, was done and it was time for goodbye. They stood for a moment on the veranda, the night breeze, redolent of the bush, cool on their faces. 'I promise I'll take good care of her, Josh,' Meredith assured him.

'I know you will. I wouldn't have asked you if I hadn't known you were capable . . . '

'You didn't always feel that way,' she complained, thinking of their first encounter. 'You almost called me an idiot to my face.'

There was a hint of amusement in his

voice when he answered. 'I was fired up.'

There was a long, almost companionable silence. 'And I didn't know who you were,' he said at last. 'You could have been a journalist.'

The threat to Cassie became real again. 'I'll ring your sister as soon as we make it,' Meredith said, more for something to say. Everything had been said before. 'She'll want to come right over.'

'And I'll call you when I get in from filming.' His voice changed. 'I wish I wasn't committed there. I should be dealing with this myself.'

'But you are. Now, you best go and get some rest or you'll spoil your good looks.'

Meredith bit her bottom lip. Your good looks! What a stupid remark to make! Embarrassed, she searched her mind for something to bridge the awkwardness.

'Although bags under your eyes wouldn't matter. The bushrangers could've been out all night robbing the coach, couldn't they? Or sitting around drinking. Probably made their own grog in a still in the bush.'

She was talking nonsense, unable to stop the flow of words. Josh Logan obviously knew how to do that. He stepped forward, gripped her shoulders and kissed her on the lips.

'Thank you, Meredith,' he said and walked away. At the end of the veranda he stopped and turned.

'I'm not married,' he said, and disappeared into the night.

Remembering, Meredith smiled. Now she knew what it was like to kiss a bearded man, an unmarried bearded man. She wondered if she'd ever see him again.

* * *

There wasn't long to wait for an answer to that, she could hear the truck coming up through the valley. Josh was on his way to the day's film location. If she

147

hurried, she could wave as he went past, to reassure him.

Carefully, she got out of bed. Better to let the child wake gradually, she decided not knowing if Cassie was grumpy in the morning. She couldn't imagine it.

The truck stopped.

The urgency of the occasion was still on Josh's tired face. Meredith felt the stirrings of foreboding. 'I'll help you load the car,' he said.

It didn't take them long. Out of habit, Meredith locked the car. Then it really was goodbye, a country goodbye — nothing said, just a casual wave to hide emotions, and he was gone.

The phone in the kitchen was ringing when she returned to the house. It was Rob. 'Are you ready to leave?' he asked, without a preamble. Already on edge, Meredith caught the anxiety in his voice.

'Give me half an hour,' she answered.

'There are a lot of people around already.'

She had to wonder if Josh and Rob weren't becoming a little paranoid — the sun was hardly up. She wanted to know were there actually any strangers among the early risers in the township, but before she could ask, he went on.

'I was going to suggest you hide Cassie on the floor under a rug until you're clear of Warrawilla. Just in case. And drive straight through. Don't stop. Not for anything.'

Rob's suggestions only fuelled her mounting fears. If both men were right, the strangers could already be in the street, asking questions. And once they came down the road to Mile End her escape would be cut off, there was no other way out.

If the threat was real, she had to hurry, to leave the house and get through the township. 'Wake up, Cassie, darling, time to get dressed,' she urged gently. The vivid blue eyes, so like her uncle's, opened at once.

Meredith made peanut butter sandwiches with the last of the bread, and, together with the contents of the fruit bowl, packed Cassie's little back-pack. She filled a water-bottle and added it to her own commodious carry-all.

'I'll take your belongings to the car while you finish your breakfast,' she said.

The small suitcase stowed, Meredith walked from the garage, her mind running through a check-list. There wasn't time to do the linen or clean the house but Rob would understand. It wasn't as if she was a dirty person. Yes, they were ready to go.

She turned her head sharply at the sound of an engine. Her heart lurched under the rib-cage. An unfamiliar car had pulled up at the gate. It could only mean one thing, the worst had happened, Cassie's grandparents had come for her.

It was too late to ask herself why Josh hadn't thought to use the discarded rusty padlock and chain on his way out. And too late to make a get-away.

Meredith didn't wait to see if the

stranger who got from the car to open the gate knew they should close it. She ran back into the house.

'Cassie, we have to go!' she called, not knowing where to, only knowing they had to move, and quickly.

She swept up the two bags from the kitchen table and, taking Cassie's hand, hurried out the back door and down the garden to the back fence. The first of the foothills loomed on the other side, thick with undergrowth.

Cassie's slight form slipped easily through the tightly-strung wires of the fence. Meredith looked on with dismay, there was no way she could squeeze through. Faced with having to climb over, she hesitated for a second, eyeing the single strand of ugly barbed-wire that topped it. She could imagine the damage it could inflict if she fell on it. Only the thought of what lay behind them spurred her on.

She threw the bags over and made a grab between the barbs. Pulling herself up, she teetered on the wire for a sickening moment before jumping, landing heavily on the hard ground.

Once amongst them, the bushes seemed skimpy cover. Meredith looked back fearfully, but the garden trees blocked her view. There was no way she could see the car or the early morning visitors. She hoped their vision was similarly restricted, at least until she and Cassie got well away. Cassie had shouldered her little back-pack and was already pushing through the under-growth and up the hillside.

10

The trees thickened as they climbed higher and Meredith began to feel safer. At the top of the first rise, she stopped, her breath rasping in her throat. From where they stood, she could see the cottage and the unfamiliar car clearly.

As she watched, a man and a woman came from the garden and got into the vehicle. She willed it to turn back toward the gate. It did the opposite. Soon it disappeared down the road to Josh's house. Not surprisingly, having come so far the strangers obviously didn't intend giving up easily.

Meredith realised she and Cassie couldn't just sit where they were. They would have to climb higher if she was to keep their pursuers in sight. Calling softly to Cassie who had found something of interest in the bush, she explained the need to go on.

'I'm not tired, Meredith,' Cassie assured her and set out to prove it, leading the way through the under-growth.

As she expected, the lovely valley with the olive trees were clearly visible from the next rise. It didn't take the strangers long to find Josh's house was empty, too. Her hopes rose as she saw them drive away, back toward her cottage. Was it too much to expect they had given up?

It was. Instead of going straight past, the car pulled up under a shady tree that commanded a clear view of the open gate at the entrance to Mile End. That meant any ideas she had of creeping back to the cottage garage and making their escape were dashed. No-one could come or go without being seen. And followed.

The two occupants of the car began unpacking rugs and cushions and what looked to be refreshments. As if they were settling in for a long wait, Meredith realised. She wondered if

Cassie grasped what was happening.

Cassie did. 'We'll have to stay up here for a long time, won't we?' she said in her matter-of-fact way.

Unwilling to admit her worst-case scenario, Meredith shrugged. 'Are you hungry? There are things to eat in your back-pack, remember.'

Cassie began to rummage in her back-pack. She offered Meredith an apple. Meredith shook her head absently, her thoughts elsewhere. She knew they couldn't remain on the hillside until nightfall waiting for Josh to return from filming.

'That was, if he did return. What if he stayed in the township with Rob, thinking she was well gone?' Or, if he came home, what if he wasn't able to persuade the visitors they were mistaken, that he knew nothing of Cassie's present whereabouts? That wouldn't be an untruth, he had no way of knowing where she was. What if he couldn't convince them and they wouldn't leave?

There were so many 'what ifs'. Too many. But she would have to do something. A long day stretched ahead.

From where they sat, she could see the layout of the foothills. It occurred to her that the township must lie beyond them. Perhaps if she and Cassie continued walking, they could get around the back of Josh's house, then up over the ridge and down the other side. To safety.

Could they do it? It was a long way for a little girl to walk. A long way for a city girl, too. Meredith looked down at her unsuitable shoes and thought of the boots she'd left behind at the cottage.

Before they set out, she needed to know for sure if she was right, and that it was possible to reach the township that way without getting lost.

'Be there, Rob,' she murmured as she reached into her bag and found her mobile phone.

The display panel showed it was out of range.

It became the worst day of Meredith's life. They made slow progress through the bush, eventually skirting Josh's house.

The morning hotted up and became noon.

'I think we'll have lunch now,' she suggested, easing her sweaty body down on to a fallen log, and slipping off her shoes to wriggle her burning toes.

The hastily-prepared peanut-butter sandwich, washed down with water, tasted surprisingly good. 'We'll keep the rest for later,' Cassie announced, re-wrapping the remainder and stowing it in her back-pack. Meredith sighed and reached for her shoes.

'Your feet are all puffed-up and red,' Cassie remarked. 'They won't fit.'

'How do you know that?'

'Uncle Josh says never to take your shoes off because it's too hard to get them on again.'

'Well, Uncle Josh is right,' Meredith said, as she struggled hopelessly to get her swollen feet back into her shoes. She gave up.

'We'll have to rest awhile until my feet cool off. Come, let's be comfortable together.'

The bed of fallen leaves on the forest floor made a soft cushion for them. Meredith pulled Cassie to her and leaned back against the moss-covered log. It felt good.

11

It was hard to know how long they slept, or what woke her. Probably her protesting body, as it cooled it stiffened into a thousand muscle aches. Cassie had no such problems. Refreshed, the little girl moved easily to gather up her back-pack. Meredith envied her resilience.

The going became harder the higher they climbed. Meredith found each throbbing footstep an effort, pausing more and more often to rest. With a wry grin, she acknowledged she was unfit, and it was too late to plan on going to the gym. But who would've thought she'd ever need this level of fitness?

They reached the top of the ridge and for a moment, the pain of her blistered feet and tired muscles disappeared. Below, she could see the little township in the valley, the first of the houses backing into the hillside.

She had been right! She might not have been able to write a novel, but she'd kept her head and won through. Nothing she'd ever done gave her more pleasure.

'It's all downhill now, sweetheart,' she cried, embracing the little girl. 'You've been wonderful. Would you like me to piggy-back you for the rest of the way?'

'Yes, please, Meredith,' Cassie replied, polite as always. Meredith crouched, the little arms went around her neck, and, as she rose with the child on her back, scratched little legs locked around her waist.

There was a gate at the end of the street for which Meredith was grateful. She didn't think she could've found the energy to climb another fence. A woman was gardening in the yard of the first house. She raised startled eyes as Meredith limped out of the bush.

'You look as though you could do

with a cuppa,' the woman said, with typical country understatement, and, after helping Cassie down, led the way indoors.

'I'd kill for one,' Meredith admitted, carefully stretching her aching back. 'But could I use your phone while you're making it?'

Rob was surprised to hear she was still in Warrawilla. 'You walked over the hill?' he asked incredulously. He cut off her explanation. 'Stay right there, I'm coming.'

The sight of the familiar figure striding up to the house shattered the control Meredith had maintained all day. She ran to his arms, and hid her face against his chest, unable to hold back the tears.

'I was wrong,' she sobbed. 'I should have gone last night when Josh asked.'

'Tell me all about it,' he murmured, picking twigs out of her tousled hair and gently smoothing it down. He listened to her somewhat muddled outline of the day's events, interrupting

161

only once to ask was Cassie all right.

'But I didn't get her away.'

'That's soon fixed,' he assured her. 'Here's what we'll do. You clean up and we'll drive out to Mile End to pick up — '

'They left the gate open, Rob,' she interrupted. 'Josh's trees — '

'So, is it Josh?'

It was a complete change of subject but Meredith knew what he was asking. She thought of Josh's vivid blue eyes with their fringe of sooty lashes. And of his darling niece. She shook her head. 'He'll be our friend, won't he?'

Rob's arms tightening around her was the only sign that he knew what her answer meant. He'd always known what she was about, from the first day she arrived in Warrawilla. They were two of a kind, they thought alike.

'Of course, especially if we save his trees,' he said, gravely.

Reminded, she cried, 'We can't go back to Mile End, they'll still be there.'

'Yes, we can and we will. As I started

to say, you clean up, cover those blisters, and I'll drive you there to get your car.' He raised an eyebrow to put an end to her protests. 'I'll look after Cassie's grandparents. It is my land after all, and if they get nasty, I will, too.'

'Meanwhile, you'll drive back here to pick up Cassie and continue on to the city.' He gazed down at her tear-stained face. 'There's still a lot of daylight left. Do you feel up to it?'

Suddenly, the idea of going home to her city apartment, and, after Cassie was gone, taking up her old life, lost its appeal. That probably meant she wouldn't see Rob Hurst again. It was a dismal thought.

She stepped out of the comfort of his arms and wiped away her tears with the back of her hand. He let her go.

'Of course, I can manage that,' she replied, lifting her chin. 'But you'll come and see me when you're next in the city, won't you?'

He frowned. 'What do you mean?'

'Even after the custody battle is over and Cassie can return to her mother, I won't be back here. I realise I'm not a country girl — '

He exploded then. 'Not a country girl? After today? You're a woman of both worlds.'

Meredith was surprised by the forceful response. Bewildered, she tried to explain. 'I was only going to be here a short while anyway . . . '

With an abrupt change of mood, Rob moved closer and put his hands on her shoulders.

'You may have thought so,' he said softly, 'but I had other ideas. It was just a matter of waiting for you to recognise where you belong.'

'And where is that?' Meredith asked with a flash of her old self.

His hands slid from her shoulders down over her back as he enveloped her in a tight embrace. 'Here, in my arms,' he said, bending his head to kiss her, gently at first and then fiercely. 'I've been wanting to do that for what seems a long, long time,' he said, at last.

She realised she'd been wanting it, too, from the first day, when he lifted his hat off his face and looked at her. That had been the beginning of their story, the once upon a time that Cassie talked about. And, like all good stories, it was ending with happy ever after, much better than any novel she could have written.

Quite unnerved by how perfect it felt, Meredith put up a shaky hand to trace the outline of his jaw under the silky beard. It was square and strong.

'This'll have to go, you know. So that I can see what you really look like.'

'As soon as the filming is over,' he promised. 'Now, go and do what you have to and then come back here — to me. I'll be waiting.'

THE END

We do hope that you have enjoyed reading this large print book.

Did you know that all of our titles are available for purchase?

We publish a wide range of high quality large print books including:
Romances, Mysteries, Classics
General Fiction
Non Fiction and Westerns

Special interest titles available in large print are:
The Little Oxford Dictionary
Music Book, Song Book
Hymn Book, Service Book

Also available from us courtesy of Oxford University Press:
Young Readers' Dictionary
(large print edition)
Young Readers' Thesaurus
(large print edition)

For further information or a free brochure, please contact us at:
Ulverscroft Large Print Books Ltd.,
The Green, Bradgate Road, Anstey,
Leicester, LE7 7FU, England.
Tel: (00 44) **0116 236 4325**
Fax: (00 44) **0116 234 0205**

Other titles in the
Linford Romance Library:

DANGEROUS FLIRTATION

Liz Fielding

Rosalind thought she had her life all mapped out — a job she loved, a thoughtful, reliable fiance . . . what more could she want? How was she to know that a handsome stranger with laughing blue eyes and a roguish grin would burst into her life, kiss her to distraction and turn her world upside down? But there was more to Jack Drayton than met the eye. He offered romance, excitement, and passion — and challenged Rosalind to accept. Dared she?

ROMANTIC LEGACY

Joyce Johnson

Wedding plans in ruins, Briony Gordon immerses herself in her job as senior wine buyer at Lapwings Wine Merchants until a dramatic turn of events forces her to reconsider her future. A substantial legacy from her beloved Grandfather gives her the incentive to explore new possibilities. At Moonwarra winery in Western Australia, Briony finds feuding brothers quarrelling over the Winery's future — a future which gives her a wonderful business opportunity and where she finds true love . . .

CONFLICT OF THE HEART

Dorothy Taylor

A summer job, as live-in nanny, caring for seven-year-old Ellie seems like a dream for Karen Carmichael. But while Ellie proves a delight, her father, archaeologist Neil Oldson is hard to get to know. Karen puts his reserve down to pressure from the looming deadline on the nearby Roman site he is managing. But when valuable finds from the site are stolen, her growing feelings for him are thrown into doubt. Then Karen's life is put in danger.

TOPAZ ISLAND

Patricia Robins

Phillida Bethel's first holiday job is mother's help to beautiful Suzanne Kingley on the exotic Topaz Island. But she could never have guessed that danger, romance, adventure and excitement are to come her way — in full measure. And her inexperience leaves her with no yardstick by which to assess the fascinating American boy, Jeff Aymon. It is the English student, Greg Somerville, who seems the only safe haven in a world of beauty which suddenly turns sinister . . .